FORENSICS
SQUAD
UNLEASHED

MONIQUE POLAK

FORENSICS SQUAD
UNLEASHED

ORCA BOOK PUBLISHERS

Library and Archives Canada Cataloguing in Publication

Polak, Monique, author
Forensics squad unleashed / Monique Polak.

Issued in print and electronic formats.
ISBN 978-1-4598-0979-6 (paperback).—ISBN 978-1-4598-0980-2 (pdf).—
ISBN 978-1-4598-0981-9 (epub)

I. Title.
PS8631.O43F67 2016   jc813'.6   c2015-904508-8
                      c2015-904509-6

First published in the United States, 2016
Library of Congress Control Number: 2015946331

Summary: Tabitha is thrilled to be attending a summer forensics camp, especially when she gets the opportunity to use her newfound skills to solve a real-life mystery in this novel for teens.

Orca Book Publishers is dedicated to preserving the environment and has printed this book on Forest Stewardship Council® certified paper.

Orca Book Publishers gratefully acknowledges the support for its publishing programs provided by the following agencies: the Government of Canada through the Canada Book Fund and the Canada Council for the Arts, and the Province of British Columbia through the BC Arts Council and the Book Publishing Tax Credit.

Cover images by Dreamstime.com
Author photo by Studio Iris

ORCA BOOK PUBLISHERS
www.orcabook.com

Printed and bound in Canada.

19 18 17 16 • 4 3 2 1

To Rachel Rudolf, former student turned good friend; Thanks for the inspiration and for bringing me to forensics camp.

ONE

"Look, let's be honest with each other. I don't like you. You don't like me. And I really wish you'd quit touching my *Junior Encyclopedia of Forensic Science.*"

Mason backs away from my bookshelf. "I didn't touch your encyclopedia. I was just looking at it."

I pick up a strand of perfectly straight, white-blond hair from the shelf and wave it at Mason. "Well, then, what do you call this?"

"Hair," Mason says, looking away. "I call it hair."

I make a snorting sound. "I call it evidence. The color, the length—approximately two and a half inches—and the lack of curl indicate that this strand of hair came from your head, Mason Johnson. Of course, we'd need to confirm with a DNA test, which is only possible if the follicle is attached. Unfortunately"—I inspect the strand—"that does not appear to be the case."

My bedroom window is open, and the warm June breeze makes the curtains rustle. Even on the third floor, where my bedroom is, the air smells of freshly mown grass—and barbecue.

I did not invite Mason over. My parents did. Dad and Mr. Johnson are partners in an accounting firm. Mom and Mrs. Johnson have known each other since high school.

"Hey, you guys, burgers are ready!" my dad bellows from the backyard. He loves barbecuing. Not just because he enjoys well-done burgers with grill marks, but because he's a neat freak. When he entertains outside, Dad doesn't have to deal with crumbs or spills.

"Honey," I hear my mom say to my dad, "you didn't leave the side door open, did you?"

"No, Lila, I didn't." I can tell from Dad's voice that he is trying not to get irritated in front of the Johnsons.

We've all got our obsessions. Dad's is cleanliness. Mom's is home security. She even uses the alarm system when we are home.

Me, I'm obsessed with forensic science.

There's a definite upside to Mom's obsession: she sells more home-security systems than anyone else in her company. When Mom meets with customers, she always mentions the time our house was broken into when the two of us were home. Apparently there is nothing like fear to generate sales.

Of course, there's a downside too. Mom is incapable of relaxing unless she is sure our house is completely secure. Even our state-of-the-art, top-of-the-line alarm system has not done the trick. It's just turned into another thing for her to stress about. Of course, Mom never mentions that part to potential customers.

Because I was only seven at the time of the break-and-enter, all I have are flashes of memory about what happened.

Mom in the kitchen making cookie batter. She offered to let me stir, but I told her I wanted to go color in my room upstairs. Trying to decide whether to color some bricks red or brown. The waxy smell of the crayons. Then hearing loud voices and strange bumping sounds. Thinking Mom had turned on the TV for company, but that she didn't usually like noisy shows. Then no more memories until a police officer with a bushy moustache came upstairs to get me.

The thieves threatened Mom with a knife and tied her to a chair. They got away with electronics and some cash. They also trashed the place, emptying drawers on the floor and smashing two porcelain lamps. They weren't in the house long. Luckily, a neighbor noticed the thieves going into our house, and she called the police. But by the time they arrived, the thieves were gone. Because they were wearing masks, Mom could not identify them. All they left were two sets of muddy footprints on our carpet. Unfortunately, they were never caught and brought to justice. That's probably why I got obsessed with forensics. After a crime happens, forensic science helps provide closure—something we never had. They say once you understand what happened, you can start putting it behind you. That's never happened for Mom.

The way Dad tells it, Mom was always a bit anxious, but the break-and-enter put her over the edge. It also inspired

Mom to give up her job as a translator and go into the home-security biz.

The picnic table creaks when Mason sits down. I take the only empty spot, which happens to be across from him. Looking at Mason makes me extra-lonesome for my BFF, Patti, who spends every summer in Cape Cod with her grandparents.

Mrs. Johnson beams at Mason and me. When she smiles, you can see almost all her teeth, including a few molars. "Have I ever told you how the two of you used to play together in our playpen? And how I always used to say you were like—"

"Salt and pepper," Mason and I say at the same time.

I don't know why Mrs. Johnson looks surprised when we finish her sentence. She has been telling the same dumb story for all of our lives—which is a little over thirteen years. "That's right, salt and pepper. Mason with that pale angel hair of his, you with those dark curls, Tabitha. We always knew you'd be close."

"We're not close," Mason says.

"That's right." I try never to agree with Mason, but sometimes I have to. "We just keep getting stuck together. Because you guys like hanging out."

"Here's to friendship!" Dad clinks his glass against Mr. Johnson's.

"To friendship!" Mr. Johnson says.

"Yes, let's toast!" Mrs. Johnson smiles and nods at Mom, as if she is a child who needs encouragement. "Let's tell the kids now!" Mrs. Johnson says.

Now Mom nods. "Tabitha, you are going to be *so* thrilled."

"We've found the *perfect* day camp for the two of you," Mrs. Johnson gushes.

"But I don't want to go to day camp." I stop myself from adding *with him*.

"Day camp is for babies."

Every summer, our parents send Mason and me to one specialty day camp or another. Last year was cooking camp (Mason's idea of heaven), the year before that was planetarium camp, the year before that was improv camp. Whatever our parents have got planned for this summer, I am not doing it. Not with Mason. Enough is enough.

Mom tries to block Dad from reaching for the saltshaker, but he reaches past her. Then she turns to me. "We've signed the two of you up for"—she pauses for dramatic effect—"forensics camp."

Mason is on his second burger. There is a ketchup smear at the corner of his mouth and burger juice dribbling down his chin. If we were inside, Dad would be coming around with paper napkins. "Are there sports?" Mason asks, without wiping away the ketchup or the burger juice. Mason detests sports.

"No team sports," Mrs. Johnson says in a sugary voice. "Just some swimming and a little fitness training. Nothing too strenuous, sweetheart. It'll be good for you."

"Swimming and fitness training?" Mason does not sound impressed.

Mrs. Johnson talks right over Mason. For once, I am interested in what she has to say. "The camp is run by the University of Montreal's Department of Forensic Science."

"What do you think, honey?" My mom is grinning at me.

"It's not fair."

Sometimes I get the feeling that Mrs. Johnson does not like me any more than I like her. When she raises her thin, arched eyebrows, they nearly disappear into the creases of her forehead. "We thought that you, of all people, Tabitha Letour, would be pleased. You've been obsessed with crime-scene investigation, well, practically forever."

"I mean it's not fair because you guys knew I didn't want to go to camp this summer, but you must've known there's no way I could resist a forensics camp. How soon does it start?"

TWO

On Monday morning Mason is sitting on the bottom step of our front stairs. His cheeks have a white film on them because he has not rubbed in his sunscreen enough. His faded Batman towel is on the step next to him.

"Listen, Mason," I say as I shut the door behind me, "my house is on your way, so I know it makes sense for us to walk together. The thing is, and I don't mean to be harsh, but, well, I think we both need to branch out. I'm looking forward to making some new friends."

Mason nods in a resigned way. "I see your point."

I tighten the straps on my backpack. "So I don't want you sticking to me like rubber cement all day. Okay?" I make a point of looking into Mason's eyes.

"Okay. Nice bracelet, by the way," Mason says.

I'm not really that into jewelry, but I do like bracelets. The one I am wearing today was a birthday present from Patti. It has black-and-white mug-shot charms.

"Hey, don't forget your towel," I remind Mason. He is always forgetting stuff. If his head wasn't attached to his neck, he'd forget that on the stairs too.

"Right. Thanks, Tabitha." Mason slings the towel over his shoulder.

It's a ten-minute walk from my house to the University of Montreal campus. At first neither of us says anything, which is fine by me. I am the opposite of a morning person.

Mason glances at me, then looks away. I get the feeling he wants to try and start another conversation. I am thinking of a way to discourage him when he clears his throat and says, "I guess you're pretty psyched about forensics camp."

"Yup." A one-word answer should indicate I am not in the mood to talk. It doesn't.

"I really loved cooking camp," Mason says.

"You're kidding."

"I'm not kidding. I still have that apron they gave us on the first day. And the chef's hat."

Sarcasm always goes right over Mason's head.

"Just don't get confused and wear that get-up to forensics camp," I say.

"I would never do that."

I sigh. "I was joking."

"Right," Mason says, "I mean, *ha-ha*."

We stop at the traffic lights at the corner of Côte-des-Neiges Street and Queen Mary Road. Someone has put up a poster offering a one-hundred-dollar reward for a missing Chihuahua. I know what I'd do with one hundred dollars. I'd buy this DNA kit I saw online. It comes with a centrifuge and an electrophoresis chamber for separating DNA strands.

Mason is studying the poster. The Chihuahua, whose name is Rexford, is looking out over the edge of a purse. He has unusually large ears for such a tiny dog. They stick up like a bat's. "Rexford looks needy," Mason says, "and that was before he got lost. Poor little guy."

I study Rexford's photo. Mason is right: there *is* something needy about the look in the dog's eyes. But I don't feel sorry for Rexford the way Mason does. To be honest, something about the dog's needy look annoys me. "Maybe they just misplaced him. In a teacup or a slipper. That dog is microscopic—even by Chihuahua standards."

It is uphill to the university gates, and Mason is out of breath when we get there. In the distance, I can see a crowd gathered outside the Life Sciences Building, where the forensics camp is being held.

Mason wipes the sweat off his forehead. "What do you think is going on over there?"

"Don't you see the yellow tape, doofus? It's a crime scene!" I tug on Mason's sleeve. I want to go investigate!

A car has been abandoned on the curb. When we get closer, we see bicycle handlebars poking out from underneath the front of the car.

"Yikes," Mason says.

A guy on a skateboard stops to take a look. "I hate to think about what happened to the dude who was riding that bike," he says.

"There's no sign of blood on the pavement," I tell him.

"Good point." The skateboarder gives me a thumbs-up before he zips off.

Mason is shaking his head. He looks a little green.

I punch his arm. "Hey, Mase, don't take it so hard. I bet you anything this whole thing is a setup for forensics camp."

Mason's face relaxes. "I hope you're right," he says.

A young woman with long, thick red hair and purple cat's-eye glasses is standing behind us. I suspect she has been listening in on our conversation. Still, I am surprised when she taps my shoulder. "Forensic scientists never make assumptions," she says. "They analyze evidence."

Before I can ask her who she is, she walks away.

We have to take an elevator to the fourth floor, where the Department of Forensic Science is. Three other kids are waiting for the elevator. I recognize a girl from school. "I'm Stacey," she says to us. "You're Tabitha, right? Patti's friend? I had a feeling you'd be at forensics camp too. You were in my second-grade class. Whenever we sang 'Who Stole the Cookies from the Cookie Jar?' you'd ask Mrs. Smitt for evidence. I didn't even know what *evidence* was."

"That sounds like Tabitha," Mason says. "By the way, I'm Mason." I roll my eyes when he shakes Stacey's hand. What thirteen-year-old shakes other kids' hands?

Mason must know what I am thinking, because he mouths the words, *I'm branching out.*

Stacey introduces us to the two other kids. "These are my cousins Muriel and Nico. They're from Vancouver."

"We're twins," Muriel says. It would not take a DNA test to figure that one out. Muriel and her brother have the same wiry build; they also have the same dark eyes and straight brown hair, though Nico's is short and Muriel's hangs in a ponytail down her back.

When we get off the elevator, we see double glass doors with white lettering that says *Department of Forensic Science*. I stop to savor the moment—I, Tabitha Letour, am about to spend a week studying forensics at a university. It's a dream come true.

Two counselors are waiting in the reception area. One is a tall broad-shouldered guy with pimples on his cheeks and nose. The other is the redheaded eavesdropper who tapped on my shoulder outside. She must have taken the stairs.

They introduce themselves. The guy's name is Lloyd Burke. The woman is Samantha Buxbaum. They are third-year forensic-science students.

"Tabitha Letour?" Samantha reads my name off the first of a stack of notebooks she is holding.

"That's me."

"Right." Samantha hands me the notebook. "We've met." I am expecting her to smile when she says that, but she doesn't. Something tells me Samantha Buxbaum is not a big smiler. "Mason Johnson?"

I lift my chin toward Mason. "That's him."

"I can tell her my own name," Mason mutters.

"Stacey Thompson. Nico Watkins. Muriel Watkins." Samantha hands them their notebooks. Still no smile.

Stacey sniffs her notebook like an airport dog sniffing for drugs. "This cover is plasticized."

"Stacey is trying to save the planet," Muriel explains.

Stacey shakes her head as if to say that saving the planet is a big responsibility for just one person. "Plastic is not biodegradable. Most of it will never disappear. Ever." She taps her notebook on the word *ever*.

Samantha has one notebook left. "That's a good point about the plastic." She whips out a small spiral notepad from the back pocket of her black pants. "I'm going to write that down so we can look into getting different notebooks next summer." Once that's done, she reads the name off the last notebook. "Nathaniel Willet?"

The elevator doors slide open, and a boy in baggy khaki-colored shorts and a T-shirt with a winged skull on it slouches out. "I'm Nathaniel," he says as he comes through the glass doors.

Lloyd rests his butt against the desk in the reception area. Samantha stands next to him and says, "Pull up some chairs." We grab chairs and make a semicircle around the two of them. "Do any of you know what the word *forensics* means?" Samantha asks.

Nathaniel does not raise his hand. "It means we're going to be examining gravesites and human skulls." His voice sounds flat—as if he examines gravesites and human skulls on a regular basis.

"Uh, I hate to disappoint you, but not exactly," Lloyd says. "Anyone else?"

I raise my hand. "Forensic science is the application of science to the law. Forensic scientists help the police, a judge or a jury understand the science used to solve a crime."

Lloyd whistles.

"Tabitha has memorized the *Junior Encyclopedia of Forensic Science*," Mason says. "She asked for it for her birthday when she was in fifth grade."

"Actually, it was fourth grade," I say.

Lloyd leans in closer to us. "One of the things we want to do this week is dispel some of the myths that surround forensic science. I'll bet most of you have watched TV shows like *CSI* and *Criminal Minds*."

"Nico and I watched all seven seasons of *Criminal Minds*," Muriel says. "Twice."

"I really wish they hadn't canceled *CSI: Miami*," Mason adds.

. I don't say anything. Even the music on crime shows upsets my mom, so I never get to watch that stuff.

"The problem with most of those shows," Lloyd says, "is that they don't portray forensic science very accurately. Can you think of any examples of what I'm talking about?"

Lloyd looks around, but none of us can answer his question. "Well, on TV," Lloyd says, "forensic scientists behave like detectives—meaning they actually solve crimes. In real life, forensic scientists stick to science. They transmit their findings to detectives who try to solve the case."

"Another difference," Samantha adds, "is that on TV, you often see one forensic scientist analyzing everything: documents, fingerprints, bones, teeth, blood splatter." Nathaniel looks up at the mention of blood splatter. "In reality," Samantha continues, "there are many different branches of forensic science, and forensic scientists work together as a team. Just like you guys will be working together this week."

Samantha points to a chart on the wall behind her and reads off some of the branches of forensic science. Forensic anthropology studies the human skeleton; forensic biology focuses on bodily fluids and DNA; forensic toxicology uses chemistry to identify substances; and fingerprint analysis looks at visible, invisible and three-dimensional prints and tries to identify whom they belong to. Forensic accounting analyzes data to assess if there has been financial fraud. I have to remember to tell my dad about that one.

Samantha turns back to us. "We want to start by emphasizing that forensic scientists need to pay close attention to details. Sometimes things that seem unimportant turn out to be extremely important. On your way in just now, you passed a simulated crime scene."

I look at Mason and raise my eyebrows. *See*, I wish I could say, *I was right. They set the whole thing up.*

I have a hunch we're going to investigate that simulation.

My hunch is confirmed when Lloyd says, "Before we can go down there, we've got to talk about what to do at a crime scene."

THREE

We each get to borrow a point-and-shoot camera. The cameras are for the university's forensic-science students, so we need to be careful not to drop them or smudge the lenses.

Stacey sighs. "Look at all this unnecessary packaging," she says as we unpack the cameras from the boxes they are stored in.

Samantha and Lloyd are going to give us a lesson in forensic photography so we can go back outside and document the crime scene.

Muriel raises her hand. "Samantha, are we also supposed to take notes?" she asks. I can tell Muriel wants to be Samantha's favorite.

"Absolutely," Samantha says. "Always have your notebook ready."

Muriel glows.

Nathaniel slouches lower in his chair and sighs loudly. "I thought this was camp. Not school."

If Samantha thinks Nathaniel is being rude, she does not let it show. "Forensic scientists don't go anywhere without their notebooks. Taking detailed notes at a crime scene is super important. Besides, this is just going to be a mini-lesson," she tells Nathaniel. "And there's no test at the end of the week…though you guys will be using forensic science to solve a case. If that's okay with you, of course." Even though Samantha's face is serious, I know she's teasing Nathaniel.

Nathaniel lifts his head. "That part sounds okay."

Nico keeps shifting in his chair, as if he can't get comfortable. "If you want us to take notes," he says, "I think you may have overlooked one small detail." He pauses. "We don't have anything to write with!"

We all laugh—even Samantha. Lloyd grabs a box from a nearby table. Inside is a packet of ballpoint pens that say *University of Montreal Department of Forensic Science* on them. I vow never to throw mine away, even when it runs out of ink.

Stacey is sitting next to me. She has opened her notebook to the first page and is making a list of all of our names.

Lloyd starts the lesson. "Like Samantha just said, recording case notes in your notebooks is extremely important. As you take notes, you want to try and answer the questions who, what, where, when and how."

"What about the why?" Muriel asks.

"I'll get to that in a minute, Muriel." Lloyd extends his arm like he is stopping traffic. "So as I was saying, forensic scientists try to figure out: *Who* was there? *What* type of crime was committed? *Where* are the boundaries of the crime scene?

When was the crime committed? And *how* was the crime committed? We don't ask *why*—that's the detectives' job."

"Always use a pen to take notes," Samantha adds. "And if you have to cross something out, make sure you initial it. Otherwise, your notes may not hold up in court. You guys got all that?"

"*Hold up in court*," Nico repeats the words to himself. "Cool!"

"All right then," Lloyd says. "Let's talk about forensic photography. What makes forensic photography so important is that it provides a permanent visual record of a crime scene. Once you move something at a crime scene, it never goes back to the way it was. So if a case goes to trial, forensic photography lets people who were not at the scene know what things looked like. Which is why forensic scientists need to take photos as soon as possible after a crime has occurred, in case evidence is moved"—Lloyd drops his voice as if he is about to tell us something terrible—"or tampered with."

Lloyd looks at Samantha. It must be her turn to talk.

"Forensic scientists need to take three kinds of photos at a crime scene." Samantha pauses, and I figure that's because she wants us to write this next part down so we'll remember it. Now I open my notebook and write the numbers 1, 2 and 3. I hope Samantha notices that my *University of Montreal Department of Forensic Science* pen is poised for note taking. Muriel is not the only one who wants to be Samantha's favorite.

"The three kinds of photos are overall, mid-range and close-up. You'll want to use your camera's wide-angle setting for overall shots." Samantha gives us a minute to find the wide-angle setting on our cameras. "When we go outside, you should try to shoot the whole street corner. That would be an example of an overall. A mid-range photo might include the car with the bicycle sticking out from underneath it. A close-up could be just the handlebars or the front tire. Remember to use the zoom for those close-ups. Can you figure out where your zoom is?" We all fiddle around with our cameras until we find the way to control the zoom.

"And keep a detailed list in your notebook of every photo you take," Lloyd says. Stacey nods. I guess she likes lists. "That way you'll avoid confusion afterward," Lloyd explains.

Muriel's arm shoots up into the air. "Why don't forensic scientists just take pictures with their cell phones? Wouldn't that be a lot easier?"

Lloyd shakes his head. "The resolution isn't high enough on a lot of cell-phone cameras. If your photograph is blurry, you risk losing important evidence. Plus your cell phone might be seized, and everything on it could be looked at in court."

"Wow, I never would have thought of that," Muriel says.

I am writing so much down, I have to shake out my wrist. Except for Nathaniel, the others are also taking tons of notes.

"I'm glad you guys are psyched about forensics camp." Samantha does not look at Nathaniel when she says that. Probably because he has just yawned and not bothered to cover his mouth. "Now that you're equipped with cameras, notebooks and pens"—Samantha glances at Nico—

"we'll head back outside. You have forty-five minutes to record your observations and take the three kinds of photographs we discussed. But before we go, we need to brief you on the facts of the case."

I open my notebook to a fresh page.

Lloyd takes the fact sheet out of a file folder and reads it to us in a solemn voice. I close my eyes, and for a moment I let myself imagine that I am a forensic scientist being briefed by a police officer.

"A cyclist was struck by a car at twenty-one hundred hours last night." I get a little thrill when Lloyd says *twenty-one hundred hours* instead of 9 PM. I know from my *Junior Encyclopedia of Forensic Science* that forensic scientists use a twenty-four-hour clock to avoid confusion. "The cyclist was taken to hospital by ambulance. The driver fled the scene on foot." Lloyd looks up at us. "Any questions?"

Mason bites his lip. "Is the cyclist all right?"

I nudge Mason. "News flash. It's a made-up case. There wasn't really a cyclist. So you don't have to worry about him."

"Actually, it's an excellent question, Mason," Samantha says. "And it also demonstrates your compassion for others." Is it my imagination, or does she shoot me a stern look when she says that? I hope she doesn't think I lack compassion for others. It's only Mason I lack compassion for. "We want you to take this case as seriously as you would a real one, and information about the victim is always important. For your information, the cyclist remains under observation at the hospital. Had he remembered to wear his helmet, he probably would have been okay."

I don't bother writing that down, though Stacey seems to be recording every word. She has the smallest handwriting I have ever seen. Maybe it's a way of saving trees. I feel slightly guilty that I am already on page three of my notebook.

When we get outside, the others crowd around the bicycle. Nico and Muriel argue as they snap photographs. Muriel elbows her brother. "Move! I'm trying to get a close-up shot."

"Me too!"

"I'm older than you are!"

"Three minutes doesn't count," Nico mutters, but I guess they do, because he moves over.

Mason and Stacey take notes. Nathaniel's notebook is open, but as far as I can tell, he has not written anything down.

"Hey, hey, no touching!" Lloyd calls out when Mason squats down and runs his fingers over the dented bike bell. "You're tampering with the evidence!"

I am the only one who thinks to check the inside of the car. Samantha is behind me, and I can sense her reading over my shoulder as I record my observations. I hope she is impressed. *Six beer bottles, four open, on the floor, passenger side.*

I take three sets of photos, including overall photos of the whole scene, mid-range photographs of the car floor and close-ups of the open beer bottles.

Afterward, when I tell the others about the beer bottles, Samantha points out that the driver might have been drinking, which could explain why he or she fled the scene.

First a missing bike helmet and now beer bottles? If you ask me, it's a suspicious combination. Forensics Camp better be about solving cases—not about life lessons for thirteen-year-olds.

The others do not seem to notice—or mind—that Samantha and Lloyd have slipped in the life lessons.

"Whose car is it anyway?" Nathaniel asks. "Once we know that, we'll know who did it."

"Not necessarily," Samantha tells him. "The police ran the license plate in their system. It turns out this car was stolen."

"Which means," Lloyd adds, "we're going to have to dust for fingerprints. Any chance you guys might be interested in learning how to do that?"

We all say *yes* or *of course* at the same time.

At improv camp, we each performed a four-minute improv act. At planetarium camp, we saw one of Saturn's rings. At cooking camp, we learned to make profiteroles.

But learning to dust for fingerprints is better than all that other stuff combined.

I might even be able to put up with a few life lessons along the way.

FOUR

We are back upstairs, sitting at a long rectangular table in the Department of Forensic Science conference room. Because our chairs swivel, we cannot resist testing them out. Nico is the only one who cannot stop. "Nico," Samantha says, but not unkindly, "if you could stop swiveling. Please. You're making me dizzy."

"Okay, sorry about that. I'll try." Nico gives his chair one last swivel.

"Solving a crime is like solving a puzzle. The pieces need to fit—and there's no use forcing them," Samantha tells us. I think about how when I was a kid, Patti and I used to try jamming puzzle pieces together. Samantha is right. It never worked.

Nathaniel is eyeing a poster showing a cross section of a skull. Nico has stopped swiveling, but now he is twirling his pen, first in one direction, then the other. Maybe I should add those things to my list of observations.

Samantha wants us to take notes about something called Locard's Exchange Principle. Edmond Locard, one of the world's first forensic scientists, lived between 1877 and 1966, and was known as France's Sherlock Holmes. "Locard's Exchange Principle states that the perpetrator of a crime will bring something into the crime scene and take something from it," Samantha explains. "Or as Locard once said, 'Every contact leaves a trace.'"

Stacey nods as if she has just learned something really deep. "It's the same with our planet," she says. "Humans use up natural resources and leave traces—like plastic waste." We already know how Stacey feels about plastic.

"That's an interesting connection," Samantha tells Stacey. "I like how you think." The compliment makes Stacey beam. I get the feeling Stacey would like Samantha to say more about how smart she is, but Samantha has material to cover. "Now let's name some of the things that can be *taken* from a crime scene," she says.

Lloyd makes two columns on the whiteboard. One says *things taken from a crime scene*, the other says *things brought into a crime scene*.

"Money can be taken," I say, "or electronics equipment." I am thinking about the time our house got broken into. Mom and Dad hardly ever mention the break-in when I'm around. All I've ever heard Mom say about it is how relieved she was the thieves never went up to the third floor, where my bedroom is.

For a second, I see myself as a little girl coloring in my room, trying to make sense of the loud noises downstairs.

Why is the sound on the TV getting louder? I have remembered this scene before, only now I see something else. The little girl—it's me, of course—is pressing her palms over her ears. Then, just like that, the picture disappears.

Lloyd writes down the words *money* and *electronics equipment*.

"If there's a kidnapping, people get taken," Muriel adds.

"Jewelry," Nico calls out, swiveling—but then stopping himself—when Lloyd adds *jewelry* to the list.

"Passports," I say. "When we're out of the country, my mom is paranoid about our passports getting stolen." Two years ago, when the three of us went for a beach holiday to Cuba, Mom was always checking her bag to make sure the passports were still there.

"Those are all good suggestions," Samantha says. "But you guys are thinking mostly about thefts. What about other kinds of crimes? I want to see you think outside the box."

Mason scratches his head. "If it's a hit-and-run, and the driver takes off from the scene, there could be paint from the car he hit on his car."

Nathaniel comes up with something too. "If it's an assault, you could get someone's blood on you," he says.

"Or fibers from their clothes," I add.

"Excellent," Samantha says. "Now, what about things that are brought *to* a crime scene?"

"Well, there's stuff like weapons"—Nathaniel closes his eyes for a second, as if he is picturing guns and knives, then opens them again—"and fingerprints," he says.

"Fingerprints on weapons," Nico adds.

"Hair." Mason looks at me. He must be remembering the strand of hair I found on my bookcase over the weekend. I shrug and give Mason a teeny smile. I want him to know I'm over it.

Thinking about Mason touching my encyclopedia reminds me how after the break-in it used to upset me knowing that strangers had handled our stuff and trashed the place—and I come up with another item for Samantha's list. "Footprints," I call out.

Lloyd rests his digital pen on the tray at the bottom of the whiteboard. "That's a great start, folks," he tells us. "As you know, we're going to discuss fingerprints first. Samantha? You want to give them some background?"

When Samantha takes over, Lloyd goes to the supply closet at the side of the room. He must be preparing something for later in the lesson.

"You've probably heard that no two people have the same fingerprints," Samantha tells us. "Not even identical twins. Fingerprints are like snowflakes. Every single print is unique."

Which is pretty amazing, considering there are over seven billion people on the planet. Not to mention all the people who used to live here, and all the ones who have not yet been born. With all those billions, you figure there might be some overlap. But no.

"What most people don't know," Samantha continues, "is that every person has ten completely different fingerprints."

Now, of course, we are all examining our fingertips.

"You'll have time for that later," Samantha promises us. "I need to cover some more theory first." She waits until we are focused on her again. "Some fingerprints are latent, others are visible, and others are three-dimensional. Latent means the fingerprints are there, but we can't see them—not until we dust for them. Visible means we can see them with the naked eye. Say someone leaves greasy prints on a window or a glass—we can see those. What do you think three-dimensional fingerprints look like?"

"Uhh, like they have three dimensions." Nico looks insulted when no one laughs.

"If someone pokes something soft with their fingers—for example, a donut with chocolate glaze on it—they would leave three-dimensional prints in the chocolate glaze," Mason says. Why am I not surprised he is thinking about donuts?

But Samantha approves of Mason's example. "The next thing you need to know is there are three kinds of fingerprint patterns—"

"Loops, whorls and arches," I say without realizing I have finished her sentence. "Oops." I cover my mouth with one hand. "That was in the *Junior Encyclopedia of Forensic Science*. Chapter four."

I'm glad that Samantha does not seem to mind my interruption. "All right then, Tabitha, why don't you go ahead and tell us what you know about loops, whorls and arches?"

I am daydreaming about how one day I want to study forensic science at the University of Montreal and maybe be a counselor at forensics camp. I picture myself at the whiteboard explaining Locard's Principle.

"Tabitha?" Samantha says.

"Oh, yeah, sorry. Loops have ridges that start at one end and go all the way around, then back to where they started. That's why they're called loops."

Samantha puts an image of a looped fingerprint on the screen at the other side of the room.

"With whorls, the ridges enter at one end, make a circle, then go out the other end. Arches make an arch. The ridges enter, then go out the other end but without circling."

Samantha is showing us more images, but I am the only one looking at the screen. The others have moved closer to the window, where the light is better for examining their fingertips. I already know some of my fingerprints are arched and the rest are whorls.

"I have a whorl!" Muriel says as if she has discovered a new planet.

"That's impossible!" Nico grabs Muriel's hand. "We're twins, and I have loops and arches."

Muriel pulls her hand away. "Didn't you hear what she just said about twins—even identical ones?"

Lloyd brings a cardboard box over to the table. When he hands us each a plain white mug, my first thought is that I am not thirsty. But we are not having drinks. The mugs must have something to do with our fingerprinting lesson.

"Touch your face with your fingers. Like this." Lloyd circles his cheeks, then runs his fingers down his nose. If he keeps doing that he is going to get even more zits. Now he grabs his mug with both hands.

We copy him. Except for the whirring sound of a fan in the corner, the room is quiet.

We set our mugs down in front of us. Samantha passes around a box of medical gloves, and we each take a pair.

Stacey pulls one glove down over her wrist. "Why are you looking at me like that?" she asks me.

"I just thought since they're made of plastic, you might…you know…say something. About the planet."

Stacey wiggles her fingers inside the gloves. "I checked the box for the list of contents. These gloves are made of nitrile rubber. It's a recyclable substance."

Samantha raises her hands up in the air. She has gloves on too. "The first reason forensic scientists wear gloves is for safety. Gloves protect us when we're handling dangerous substances. But there's another reason. Gloves prevent us from contaminating our evidence."

Lloyd hands Samantha a tray with a bowl of fine black powder in it and some wands that look like a cross between fountain pens and the kind of brush my mom uses to powder her face. Samantha holds the tip of the wand over the bowl to collect the powder. "Both the powder and the wands are magnetic, so you don't need to dip the wand in the powder."

Then Samantha squeezes the handle at the top of the wand. That releases the black powder, which drifts down and sticks to the places where she held her mug. "Be careful not to let the wand touch the fingerprints, or you might lose some of the detail in the print," she warns us.

"Super cool!" Nico says when Samantha's fingerprints emerge from the white background.

We each get to dust our mugs for our fingerprints. But that turns out to be only step one of our fingerprinting lesson.

"You don't want to lose your evidence," Lloyd explains. "This is where you'll need your cameras again."

Samantha and Lloyd take out their cameras and show us how to get clear close-up shots of our fingerprints.

I move in until all that appears in my camera screen is the mug with my fingerprints.

"Hey, we're taking *mug* shots!" Nico calls out.

This time everyone laughs—except Nathaniel. He could be the grumpiest kid I've ever met.

Taking photographs is not the only way to record fingerprint evidence. Lloyd demonstrates how to use special sticky tape to lift his prints from the mug he used. "This tape costs thirty bucks a roll," he tells us, "so don't waste it. Smooth the tape out with your thumb like this," he says, "so you don't get any creases or air bubbles. And when you're done, always fold the tape over at the end. You don't want to spend half an hour at a crime scene looking for the start of your tape." I write that down in my notebook and underline it twice. It is the kind of information I could never find in the *Junior Encyclopedia of Forensic Science*.

Lloyd presses the sticky tape down on an index card, then writes out his name in block letters along the top of the card, last name first.

"Is this how the police do it?" Stacey asks as she tears off a piece of sticky tape from the roll.

"Basically, yes," Lloyd answers. "Of course, the police also enter their evidence on computers. We won't be doing that this week. So I'm curious...any of you interested in becoming forensic scientists—or police officers?"

Nathaniel looks up from his index card. "My dad's a cop."

"You didn't answer Lloyd's question," I tell Nathaniel.

"I said, 'My dad's a cop.'"

"My dad is an accountant," I say. "So is Mason's. That doesn't mean we want to be accountants, does it, Mason?"

"I want to be a pastry chef," Mason says.

Nathaniel blows some leftover dust off his mug. "Of course I want to be a cop." As if there could be any doubt.

"Well, I've always wanted to be a forensic scientist," I say.

Mason's eyes are darting back and forth between Nathaniel and me. "Tabitha knows more about forensic science than any kid I ever met," he says. Mason's admiring tone makes me feel slightly guilty. Mason is annoying, there's no question about it. But I suppose I could try being a *touch* nicer to him.

"Are you two best friends?" Muriel asks us.

That makes us both laugh.

"Kind of," Mason says.

"Not exact—" I catch myself before correcting him. "It's complicated," I say instead—besides, it's the truth.

"Tabitha's best friend is this girl named Patti," Stacey says.

Muriel turns to Nathaniel. "So is that why you came to forensics camp? Because you want to be a cop one day like your dad?"

Nathaniel looks over at the poster of the skulls. Something tells me he would rather be hanging out with them than with us. "To be honest, I didn't want to go to any kind of camp. My parents needed me out of their way this week."

"How come?" Muriel asks.

"Are they getting the floors done?" Nico chimes in. "We had to stay with our neighbors when we had our floors redone."

Nathaniel has not taken his eyes off the poster. "I don't want to talk about it."

Samantha looks up from collecting the wands and magnetic dust. "Whatever the reason is, we're glad to have you here, Nathaniel." I think she is trying to send Muriel and Nico the message that they should quit asking Nathaniel personal questions.

But Muriel does not quit. She may not be tactful, but she has advanced interrogation skills. "Is someone sick? Or did someone die? Is that why you'd rather not talk about it?"

Nathaniel shakes his head. "Not quite, but it's almost as bad. Look, if you really want to know"—he finally stops looking at the poster—"my grandmother is getting married on Saturday."

"What's so bad about that?" I ask. "Weddings are fun."

"There's usually cake with buttercream frosting," Mason adds. He gets a faraway look in his eyes when he mentions frosting.

Nathaniel scowls. "My grandmother is seventy-one. That's too old to get married. It's embarrassing. What's even worse is she's marrying some guy she met at her bereavement group. She went there to mourn my grandpa—not to meet his replacement!"

Lloyd takes the magnetic powder from Samantha and empties it into a glass container. Samantha puts the wands away in a drawer.

Lloyd blows some magnetic powder off his fingers, then looks up at Nathaniel. "I'm sure no one could ever replace your grandpa," he says softly.

"You're right about that. My grandpa is"—Nathaniel sucks in his breath—"*was* really cool."

"Some stuff just takes getting used to," Lloyd adds. I cannot tell whether the advice is for Nathaniel or if Lloyd is speaking from experience.

Samantha watches Lloyd. When she clears her throat, I know it's because she wants to get us back on track. I don't think Samantha enjoys talking about feelings. She prefers facts. I'm like that too. "Now that we've put all the fingerprinting equipment away, it's time to talk about tomorrow. That's when Lloyd and I are going to tell you about the case that will be the focus of the rest of forensics camp."

Nathaniel is back to slouching in his chair. "So are we ever going to find out who hit the cyclist?"

"I'm afraid not," Samantha says. "That was just a mock crime scene to introduce forensic photography, fingerprinting and note taking."

When Nathaniel groans, Lloyd does that thing he does with his arm—extending it like he's a traffic cop at a busy corner. "Think of that bicycle case as the preview before the main attraction," he says.

Nathaniel's cell phone vibrates in his pocket. "I hate that noise," he mutters.

"You can fix it," Muriel tells him. "If you don't like the steady pulse, you can adjust it. It's under *Settings*. Want me to show you?"

"My sister knows everything about cell phones and computers," Nico says. "Unfortunately, she was not blessed with my sense of humor."

Muriel rolls her eyes. "You make enough bad jokes for the whole family. Including Stacey's side."

Nathaniel's cell phone vibrates again.

"Don't you want to see who's calling?" Muriel asks. "What if it's about the wedding?"

Nathaniel shrugs. "What if it is?"

My parents are always saying I need to work on developing my emotional intelligence. They should meet Nathaniel. Compared to him, I'm an emotional Einstein.

FIVE

From the outside, our house looks a bit like a prison. An eight-foot fence barricades the property, and there are iron bars over the basement windows. When the house was broken into, the thieves got in through the basement. If the city would allow it, I'm sure Mom would put barbed wire at the top of the fence.

"It's me," I call when I unlock the front door and tap in the security code for the alarm. I am so used to announcing myself, I do it even when nobody is home. "Mom? Dad?"

I expect my parents to be waiting, eager to hear about my first day at forensics camp. But nobody answers. I kick off my sandals. There is still no sign of Mom or Dad, and I can't help feeling a little lonesome.

Dad's car is in the driveway, so he must be back from work. Maybe they went for a walk. Mom's boss is so happy with her sales numbers, he agreed to let her work from home three days a week. The only problem with the new arrangement is that she isn't getting as much exercise now that she isn't walking to her office as often. Which is why she's been badgering Dad to join her for walks on her at-home days.

I leave my backpack on the floor and head for the kitchen, where I open the fridge. How can a fridge be so full and yet have nothing in it that I feel like eating? Cheese? Red grapes? Greek yogurt? Nah. I'm in the mood for chocolate pudding or tortilla chips dunked in salsa. But ever since Dad was diagnosed with high blood pressure, Mom's been shopping strictly according to the Heart and Stroke Foundation guidelines. There's a *Canada's Food Guide* poster on the fridge door. I grab a pen from the counter and write *SALSA* in the vegetable area.

That's when I hear the music. It's thin and reedy-sounding, like it's coming from a snake charmer's flute. Definitely not the soft rock my parents usually listen to. For a moment, I stand in the kitchen and listen. I am trying to decide whether I like or hate the sound. I think I am closer to hating it.

I follow the music downstairs to the den. The air smells sweet and sort of powdery. What is going on down there?

"Mom? Dad?"

They do not answer.

My parents are sitting across from each other on the rug, an ivory candle in a brass candleholder between them. Their legs are folded under them; their hands rest in their laps.

"Tabitha!" Mom says, popping up from the rug. "You startled me!"

The powdery smell is coming from a cone of incense burning on the mantel.

I could apologize, but I don't. I haven't done anything wrong. "What are you guys doing?" I ask.

Mom has gotten back into position. She takes a deep breath in, then exhales loudly. "Your father wanted us to try meditating."

"It's harder than it looks," Dad says, getting up to give me a hug. He is still wearing his work clothes, and his shirt feels stiff against my face. "Tell us all about forensics camp," he says into my hair.

I stay by the door. I am afraid that if I walk into the den, my parents will try to make me meditate too. "It was cool. We learned how to do forensic photography and dust for finger-prints. Tomorrow we're getting a case to solve. Hey, Dad, did you know there was something called *forensic accounting*?"

"I've heard of it. But they certainly didn't offer that sort of thing when I was at university. If they did, I'd have signed up," Dad says.

Mom lets her hands hover by her sides, thumbs and index fingers touching.

"How did Mason like forensics camp?" Dad asks. He sits back down across from Mom and does the same weird thing with his fingers.

"I guess he liked it. If you don't mind my asking—why are you guys doing that thing with your fingers?"

"It's called the Gyan Mudra," Dad says. "Your mother and I just watched a DVD about meditation, and we learned how to do it."

"The Gyan Mudra is supposed to generate wisdom and calmness," my mom adds.

Calmness? That explains it. Meditating must be Dad's latest scheme to help Mom chill out. And, knowing Mom, she's probably hoping that meditation will help reduce Dad's blood pressure. It is probably not a good time to point out that so far the Gyan Mudra does not seem to be working.

"Maybe you'd like to try meditating sometime too. We could all stand to mellow out a bit," Dad says. "Meditating could be a family activity."

I take two steps back. "Going to the beach is a family activity. Skiing is a family activity. Meditating is *not* a family activity. I think I'll go up to my room and read. That's my way of *mellowing out*."

For people who are supposed to be meditating, my mom and dad are talking an awful lot. I hear them as I go upstairs. "I don't know where Tabitha gets that harshness," my dad is saying. "Neither of us is harsh."

"Maybe the forensics camp wasn't the best idea after all. Maybe it's dredging stuff up for her from—" Mom drops her voice, which is how I know she must be talking about the break-in. Though the subject comes up a lot when she talks to clients, she avoids it when I'm around. I think she is afraid it might upset me. Which it kind of does, but less and less as time goes on.

"The meditating might help," my dad says.

"I don't think I like meditating," Mom says. "It makes me anxious."

My dad laughs. Not a happy laugh. A worn-out laugh. "We have to give it a try, Lila. You need to learn to relax—not only for yourself, but for me and Tabitha. We need you—even if we don't always show it."

I stop on the stairs and think about what my dad just said. I know I can be harsh—and the part about needing my mom feels true too. But that only makes me mad. I hate feeling needy. Maybe that's why I try not to show it.

Needy. Wasn't that the word Mason used to describe the Chihuahua on the poster? Rexford. The dog who went missing. I remember Rexford's small sad eyes. Am I really like that?

And then I get a brilliant idea. I take the stairs back down to the basement two at a time and throw open the door to the den. Dad has turned off the flute music and blown out the candle. He is scooping up the ashes from the incense burner.

"You know what might help us all relax—even more than meditation? A dog!"

Dad rubs his eyes the way he does when he is waking up in the morning. "Dogs shed," he says. "And drool and scratch the floors. You know how fussy I am about the house."

"What if I'd clean up after it?" I say.

"And who'd walk the dog?" Dad asks.

"Uh, me, I guess. And if you and Mom wanted to, it would be a great way to get some more exercise."

"Tabitha is right about the exercise," Mom says. "And a dog would be company for her, but who'd look after the dog if we're out of town?"

Luckily, I have an answer for that too. "We could ask the Johnsons. I bet Mason would love to look after a dog."

And then I have a brilliant idea. I borrow Mom's number-one sales technique—fear. "I wasn't thinking so much about a companion. I was thinking we could get a *guard dog*. For protection."

They do not say no. With my parents, that just might mean the answer is yes.

SIX

When Mason and I show up for day two of forensics camp, Samantha and Lloyd are in the lobby, looking at a poster by the elevator. Another dog has gone missing. This one is a white standard poodle named Ringo.

I want to tell Samantha and Lloyd about the missing Chihuahua, and also that we might be getting a dog, but then the other kids turn up and there isn't time.

"Before we get started today, we thought we'd show you where the university cafeteria is," Lloyd tells us. "Because it's summer and there are fewer students in the building, the cafeteria is on summer hours through August. If you want to buy something to eat, it's only open in the morning from seven to nine and for lunch between twelve and one thirty. It's just down this hallway."

"I figured that out already," Stacey says, sniffing the air as we follow the counselors down the hall. When I look at her, she explains, "I smell toast. My mom says I must've been a dog in my last life."

That is another opening for me to tell everyone we might be getting a dog, but Samantha is explaining stuff again. I hope I get a chance soon to tell the others my news. "A forensic scientist needs a good nose," Samantha is saying.

Nathaniel crinkles his nose. "Not if there are corpses around." He is wearing another skull-and-crossbones T-shirt. I wonder if he has a collection.

Thinking about collections makes me twirl my bracelet. The one I am wearing today has a tiny magnifying glass dangling from it.

"How come you're so obsessed with corpses?" I ask Nathaniel.

"No reason." Nathaniel does not make eye contact when he says that. Which is why I decide there must be a reason.

"Quit bumping into me like that!" Muriel tells Nico. I thought twins were supposed to get along. After all, they shared tight quarters for nine months. But Nico and Muriel never stop squabbling.

Nico jabs Muriel with his elbow. "You're the one who keeps bumping into me."

Muriel jabs him back—a little harder than she has to.

Lloyd slows down so he can walk between them. "So what do you guys think of Montreal?" he asks.

"We miss seeing mountains," Muriel says.

"We don't miss the rain," Nico adds.

I would not expect two kids who fight so much to use the word *we* like that.

Mason is walking behind Nathaniel and me. "Most cafeteria food sucks," Mason says to no one in particular. It does not seem to bother him when no one responds. Mason is low-maintenance that way. If it was me, I'd feel ignored.

"I don't know why they think we need to see the cafeteria," Nathaniel grumbles. "We're supposed to bring our own snacks and lunches. Besides, I checked the schedule online. This morning we're supposed to learn about the case we're solving this week. The schedule doesn't mention anything about a cafeteria tour."

Mason has a one-track mind. "Now that I think about it, I have tasted some decent cafeteria food. Our school cafeteria has amazing oatmeal cookies. They've got raisins—and chocolate chips. Raisins and chocolate chips go really well together."

Samantha comes to walk beside Mason. "The pizza is pretty good at this cafeteria," she tells him. Then she taps Nathaniel's shoulder. "Just so you know, we'll be assigning you your case soon enough. We just figured this is a big campus and you'd want to know your way around."

Am I the only one who gets tingles on the insides of my elbows when Samantha says *assigning you your case*?

Everything about the Life Sciences Building is shiny and new and either chrome or white, so I am expecting more of that when Lloyd opens the double doors to the cafeteria.

What I do not expect is for Nico to slip on the tile floor. When he does, he grabs on to Muriel, and she goes flying to the floor too. Why is the floor so slippery?

What I also do not expect is the stench. Before, Stacey said she could smell toast. But there is no toast smell now. Instead, the air smells like rotten eggs.

Nathaniel gags. "Did somebody croak in here?" he manages to say. For once, I do not think he is being morbid. Not that I have ever smelled a corpse, but if I did, I would not be surprised if it smelled like this.

Mason pinches his nose. "I don't think I'll ever want to buy food from here," he says in a nasal, disappointed voice.

Stacey bends down and slides one fingertip along the tile floor, which is covered in something slick and yellow. She sniffs her finger once, twice. I can almost see her dog brain trying to identify the smell. "French-fry grease," she says, looking up at the rest of us. "Someone must have dumped a grease trap on the floor."

"A what?" Nico asks.

"A grease trap. It catches grease so the pipes don't get clogged," Stacey says. "My dad manages a fast-food restaurant. I've helped him clean out the grease trap loads of times."

"Now why would anyone go and dump a grease trap on the floor?" Samantha wonders out loud.

An Asian woman wearing a white apron and a hairnet comes running out of the kitchen at the back of the cafeteria. "Someone has made terrible, terrible mess in my kitchen!" she shouts.

Samantha grabs hold of the woman's elbow. "Be careful, Mrs. Lu! You could slip on the floor!"

Mrs. Lu just keeps saying, "Terrible mess," over and over again.

It's Lloyd who notices that Mrs. Lu is carrying a black-ened metal pan. "Where'd you get that?" he asks her.

"I found it over there," she says, pointing to the slippery floor. "When I came into the cafeteria."

Lloyd groans. "It's the grease trap," he says to Samantha in a low voice. "I think she washed it."

"Of course I washed it," Mrs. Lu says. "The grease trap was covered in oil and greasy fingerprints. I used bleach," she adds proudly.

Lloyd shakes his head when Mrs. Lu mentions the greasy fingerprints. I don't know why he cares so much about a grease trap. "All right then, let's have a look in the kitchen," he says to us, "and see what Mrs. Lu is so upset about."

The closer we come to the kitchen, the worse the smell gets. Now even Stacey is pinching her nose.

When we swing open the metal doors, we figure out where the stench is coming from.

The giant freezer doors are wide-open, and someone has dumped food all over the counters and on the floor.

A slab of shrink-wrapped beef and several packages of fish fillets are defrosting in gooey puddles. Someone has used mustard to write out the words *Beets not Meets* on the long counter. I assume whoever wrote it meant *Meats*. Either the person who left the message is a bad speller or writing with mustard is hard to do. Or both.

Stacey puts her hands on her hips. "It's too bad we can't compost any of this," she says. "If you compost meat and fish, you risk attracting rats." Stacey turns to Mrs. Lu, who has followed us back into the kitchen. "Where do you keep the garbage bags?"

"Whoa!" Lloyd extends his arm traffic-cop style again. "Not so fast!"

"What do you mean?" Stacey says. "This place is a disaster. We should help Mrs. Lu clean up. It won't take long if we all pitch in."

"I'm afraid that would be tampering with the evidence." I can see Lloyd is trying not to smile.

"Tampering with the evidence?" Mason's forehead crinkles up the way it does when he is trying to figure something out.

"That's right," Lloyd says, "the evidence." Now he's definitely smiling.

As usual, Samantha's face is perfectly serious. "You know that case you guys are going to try to solve this week?" she asks us. "You just walked in on it."

So that's why Lloyd got upset when Mrs. Lu told him she'd scrubbed the grease trap.

"I really wish you hadn't done that," I overhear Samantha tell Mrs. Lu a few minutes later.

Mrs. Lu hangs her head. "I'm very sorry. But when I saw how dirty that grease trap was, I forgot about the plan."

I understand how Mrs. Lu feels. If my dad was around, he'd have scrubbed that grease trap too.

SEVEN

A guy from building services shows up, talking on a walkie-talkie. "I'm looking into it right now," he assures whoever is on the other end of the line.

"You two work for the forensics camp, right?" he says to Samantha and Lloyd. "I understand this mess has something to do with your camp, but people from two floors up are complaining about the odor. You're going to have to get rid of that"—he grimaces when he points to the spoiled food—"now."

Samantha's purple glasses have slipped down her nose. As she adjusts them, she looks straight at the building-services worker. "You're going to have to give us an hour," Samantha says. "Our forensic scientists in training need to document the scene before anything gets touched or moved around."

Samantha's firm tone works on the guy. "Forensic scientists in training, hey? That's a mouthful." He checks the time on his watch. "One hour," he tells Samantha. "But no longer than that. And you'd better open some windows—air out the place. Sheesh, does it ever stink!"

The windows are high up, so Nathaniel, who is the tallest, goes to open the nearest one. Lloyd stops him. "Not just yet, Nathaniel. We won't touch those windows…not before you guys have some idea how the vandal got into the cafeteria."

Lloyd and Samantha explain that we'll be working in pairs, the way real forensic scientists do. One team will be responsible for taking photographs, one for taking detailed notes, and one for collecting fingerprints and miscellaneous evidence. "What's important to remember is that this is going to be a team effort. You need to work together to solve this case," Lloyd says. He makes a point of looking at the twins and also at Mason and me. "A positive attitude"—Lloyd directs this comment to Nathaniel—"benefits the entire team."

"Wanna be fingerprinting partners?" I ask Muriel. Something tells me she could use a break from her brother.

Nico and Stacey partner up. They are cousins, and I guess Nico doesn't mind hearing about environmental disaster, and Stacey likes corny jokes. They are going to be our note takers. Note taking is the perfect job for a person who likes lists as much as Stacey does.

"That leaves me and you for the forensic photo team," Nathaniel says to Mason.

Mason looks pleased. "Sure, I'll be your partner."

Nathaniel makes a noise somewhere between a grunt and a laugh. "I wasn't asking you to be my partner. I was just saying there was only us left."

I nudge Nathaniel. "Hey," I say. "Play nice."

Mason looks surprised that I've come to his defense. To be honest, I'm a little surprised myself. I know I can be hard on Mason, but it's different in our case. We've got history. Nathaniel only met him this week. He hasn't earned the right to pick on him yet.

"All right then," Nathaniel says to Mason. "Let's be partners."

"Okay," Mason says, and he gives Nathaniel a shy smile. Nathaniel smiles back. All that smiling bugs me, but I'm not sure why. I guess, in my own way, I'm possessive about Mason.

Mason and Nathaniel go upstairs to the Department of Forensic Science with Samantha for supplies. Lloyd wants the rest of us to begin by looking for signs of forced entry. "Check the windows and doors. Keep your eyes peeled for anything unusual. Remember: don't touch anything until you've got your gloves on. And keep those notebooks handy."

Muriel and I peer up at the windows. We do not see any shattered glass or cut screens. Stacey has compiled a list of all the possible points of entrance into the cafeteria. She and Nico report that the doors look normal too.

Once Samantha and the boys come back with the cameras, a box of gloves, magnetic powder, wands, tape, cue cards and brown paper bags for collecting evidence, we get down to real work.

"Forty-nine minutes," Lloyd tells us, "before we need to toss the meat and fish. I need the photography and finger-printing teams over here. Don't bother trying to get prints off the meat or the fish. The surfaces aren't flat enough, and they're way too wet. It's too bad about the grease trap. You'd have got some good fingerprints there."

Now that they have their gloves on, Stacey and Nico are testing the handles and locks on the doors to the cafeteria, checking to see if they have been tampered with. "The locks seem normal," Stacey calls out.

"You could say we've got this part of the investigation all *locked* up!" This time, we are all too busy to laugh (or groan) at Nico's joke. We are down to about forty-five minutes—and there's still a lot to do.

Mason and Nathaniel are photographing the spoiled food. Samantha reminds them that when they are done, they need to get to the four corners of the cafeteria for some overall shots.

Nico and Stacey are recording information in their notebooks—the weight of the meat and fish packages and their condition. "This five-pound package of beef is completely thawed," I hear Stacey tell Nico.

"Good observation, Stacey!" Lloyd says. "That kind of information could help us determine what time the vandalism occurred. With no air-conditioning in here, things probably defrosted pretty quickly."

Maybe our noses are getting used to the smell, or maybe it is because we are so focused on our jobs, but the smell is not as gross as before.

Muriel and I spot fingerprints on the counter and on the handle of the freezer door. "See," I say to Muriel when two thumbprints emerge from the magnetic powder we have dusted on the edge of the counter, "these ones are both arched. There's another thumbprint over there." I point to a spot a few inches away. "That one goes around in a continuous circle. Let's dust there next."

"Twenty-six minutes left!" Samantha calls out as she hands Muriel the tape and cards for lifting the fingerprints. Dusting for prints is not as easy as it sounds—and the time pressure makes it harder. Those first two thumbprints are nice and clear, but some of the other fingerprints on the counter are already smudged, making it hard to see the tiny identifying ridge details. My hands feel hot and sticky inside the rubber gloves.

Stacey is at the counter too, looking at the mustard words. "What about the message?" she asks Samantha. "Do you think building services will want to wash this up too?"

"Good point," Samantha says. "Mason! Nathaniel! We need lots of pics of the mustard message. Mid-range and close-ups, please."

My eyes are tearing up, so I grab a Kleenex from my pocket and blow my nose. I am about to throw the Kleenex into the garbage when I spot the mustard container. It is one of those squirt jars, making it perfect for writing with. "Hey, come see what I just found!" I call out to the others.

Mason takes several photographs of the mustard container. Then, once Samantha gives me the go-ahead, I fish it out of the garbage. There's a paper coffee cup next to the mustard container, so Muriel and I decide to collect that too. Muriel hands me two brown bags for collecting evidence. The counselors have already explained that it is important to store pieces of evidence separately—it is another way to avoid contamination. Muriel labels the first bag, marking the date, time and contents. Then she seals it with red tape.

Lloyd crouches down to examine the tile floor. Because it is so oily, there are lots of footprints—including ours. "Boys!" Lloyd calls Mason and Nathaniel over. "We'll need some photographs of the floor too. It looks to me like we might have some useful footwear evidence." Lloyd checks the time. "Better hurry—we're down to six minutes!"

"Footwear evidence?" Muriel looks up from the second brown bag she is labeling. "I know fingerprints are like snowflakes—everyone's are different. But I didn't know footwear was important too…"

"Footwear tells stories," Samantha says. "And Lloyd just happens to be the forensic department's footwear impression guy. That's why we call him FIG for short."

"FIG?" Lloyd says with a laugh. "No one ever told me that before. But I think I like it. FIG." He says the word to himself as if he is trying it on to see if it fits.

The man from building services turns up exactly on time. Mrs. Lu is with him, as well as two other cleaners. "Let's start by getting those windows open!" the building-services guy tells one of them. Mrs. Lu dips her mop into her bucket, and I can feel her watching us, waiting for us to leave the cafeteria so she can begin cleaning the floor.

Mason and Nathaniel are still photographing the scene. "Okay, forensic photography team, we're done here!" Samantha tells them.

Nathaniel leans down to snap one last photograph of the cafeteria floor. Nico must not be worried about getting grease on his clothes, because he drops to the floor. Then he stretches out on his side, waves his hands and sticks out his tongue. "Photo bomb!" he shouts. I am starting to wonder whether Nico ever takes anything seriously.

We head back up to the conference room to have our snacks and watch a video. Samantha tosses Nico a pair of gray shorts and a T-shirt. "They're from the lost and found," she explains. "But at least they're clean. The chair of the department would have our heads if you got grease on the furniture."

Nico's eyes light up, and I brace myself for another bad joke. "So you're saying the chair is worried about her chairs?" he asks.

Lloyd groans.

"Don't encourage him," Samantha tells him.

Stacey predicts the video will be about analyzing footwear evidence. Muriel hopes it will have something to do with digital forensic science. "That's when forensic scientists look for evidence on people's computers," she says.

Mason sits across from me at the conference table. He sighs when he sees what his mom has packed for his snack: a baggie of celery and carrot sticks. He eyes my slice of lemon pound cake. "Any chance you'd want to trade?"

"Not a chance. But thanks for asking."

Mason crunches on a celery stick. "Celery has no flavor," he says after he's eaten it.

I break off a chunk of pound cake and hand it to him.

"Hey, thanks." Mason pops the cake into his mouth.

Nico is back from the bathroom, dressed in the fresh clothes, which are a little baggy. Stacey and her cousins have the same snack: cubes of cheddar and apple slices. Only Stacey's are packed in separate reusable containers.

"I can't stand when different foods touch each other," she says when she catches me watching her.

The video is stored on a memory card. Samantha has trouble getting the card into the forensic department's laptop. She fiddles with the card, turning it upside down and trying it that way, but it is still not sliding in the way it should. Then she tries another hub, but that one is too narrow. "Hmm, I don't know what the problem is," she mutters to herself.

"Let me try," Lloyd offers, only he cannot get the card into any of the hubs either.

Muriel watches them as she pops a cube of cheddar into her mouth. "There could be some dust in there," she says after she has swallowed the cheese. "D'you want me to try something?"

"It's all yours," Samantha says, stepping away from the laptop to make room for Muriel.

Lloyd hands Muriel the memory card, which she inspects carefully. Then she crouches down so her face is level with the side of the laptop and blows into the second hub. When she tries inserting the card, it slides right in. "Ta-da!" she says. "The SD card hub was clogged. It happens sometimes, especially if a computer hasn't been used in a while."

"Thanks for the save, Muriel." Then Lloyd turns to Samantha and shrugs. "Can you believe we couldn't figure that out?"

"I know," Samantha says. "It's humiliating. And she's only thirteen. Do you realize that in twenty years these kids could be leaders in the field of forensics? We could end up taking orders from them!"

So what if Muriel solved the problem? I still feel proud. After all, I'm one of those future leaders Samantha is talking about.

EIGHT

It's obvious the video is homemade. It has no title or music, and at first the screen is hazy, and all we can hear is a buzzing that hurts my ears.

But then a round face appears from out of the haze. Mrs. Lu is sitting at a desk in what looks like a small office, talking to someone, though we cannot see—or hear—who that someone is. Whoever is filming is not doing a very good job, because the image wobbles. The words *Ming Lu, cafeteria employee*, appear in white block letters at the bottom of the screen.

Mrs. Lu's face is shiny with sweat. She is not wearing her hairnet. Instead, her black hair is tied back in a red bandanna; a few gray hairs poke out at the front. I did not notice before how high her cheekbones are. "I did not vandalize the cafeteria." Mrs. Lu's shoulders are straight, and she sounds upset, as if she is insulted that anyone would accuse her of committing a crime.

"I don't get it!" Nico says to his sister. "When did they have time to make a movie? The cafeteria just got vandalized last night."

"It wasn't really vandalized, silly," she tells him.

"Shhh," Stacey says to Muriel. "We're trying to listen."

Mrs. Lu stares right into the camera. "Why would I make more work for myself? I have to clean too much already. Those students who come to the cafeteria—not the kids at forensics camp; those ones seem okay to me—I mean the university students. They do not clean their tables. They leave garbage all over the place. And what bothers me even more is that they do not say *good morning* or *thank you* to me. Never! They treat me like I am—what is the word in English?—invisible." Mrs. Lu smacks the desk when she finds the right word. "I do not like my job very much, but I am still proud of the hard work I do. In any case, I cannot quit. I need money to support my family." Her dark eyes soften when she mentions her family. I don't think Mrs. Lu is making this stuff up.

Offscreen, we can hear a woman's voice—could it be Samantha's?—ask Mrs. Lu, "If the cafeteria smelled so bad that it needed to be closed, wouldn't that mean you'd get a few days off from work?"

"That is possible," Mrs. Lu says, shaking one finger in the air. "And they would have to pay me too—which would be very nice. Like a holiday."

The screen goes gray again. Nico pops up from his swivel chair. "Guilty!" he calls out. "Mrs. Lu even looks guilty! I could see it in her eyes!"

"Nico," Samantha says, "sit down right now! You seem to have forgotten something. Forensic scientists"—she empha-sizes the word *scientists*—"never, ever jump to conclusions. They base their findings strictly on scientific evidence. There is nothing scientific about your observation that Mrs. Lu looks guilty." I have never seen Samantha's cheeks get red before. I think she is finding her job a bit challenging.

"Okay, okay." I can tell from the way Nico is gripping the arms of his chair that he wants to swivel. "I'm just really getting into this."

"Getting into it is good," Lloyd tells him, "but jumping to conclusions—not so much."

Next up is a middle-aged guy wearing a chef's hat. He has a craggy face and a long thin nose. From the informa-tion at the bottom of the screen, we learn that this is Leo Tessier, head chef at the university cafeteria. Leo Tessier has a thick handlebar moustache and a small neat beard. Like Mrs. Lu, he begins by denying he had anything to do with the vandalism. Unlike Mrs. Lu, he does not look at the camera when he speaks.

"See how he's not making eye contact?" Nathaniel says. "That's suspicious!"

"Nathaniel!" Lloyd says sharply. "What did Samantha and I just say about jumping to conclusions before you collect and analyze your evidence?"

Leo Tessier speaks with a French-from-France accent. "Eet ees true," he says, twirling one end of his moustache (I don't say anything about that, though it strikes me as slightly fake and suspicious), "that it was not my dream to be head chef at a cafeteria." His head drops a little when he admits this. "I always thought I would be head chef at a great *restaurant*"—he switches to French to say the word *restaurant*—"a Michelin three-star *restaurant*. That was my life's ambition. But it does not mean I do not cook like a great French-trained chef. The students adore my *rôti de boeuf*, my roast beef, and on Fridays, my *sole amandine* never fails to sell out.

"My only complaint is that I work too much—all the time, nonstop. If I had a day off during the week, I would have time to apply for a better job." Chef Tessier closes his eyes as if he is imagining himself preparing *rôti de boeuf* and *sole amandine* in one of those three-star *restaurants*. When he opens his eyes again, he looks sad, and I notice the baggy skin under his eyes. "Zee smell in zee cafeteria. *Epouvantable!* Awful! We will have to close the cafeteria for at least three days to air it out. Perhaps four."

If anyone else thinks the chef did it, they are not saying. I guess we all figure it is better to keep our hunches to ourselves than get lectured by Samantha and Lloyd.

Our next suspect is Amelia Lester, the assistant chef. The first thing I notice is that her hair is the same color as Samantha's—only Amelia has dreadlocks. Her blouse has puffed sleeves—it looks like it probably came from a vintage shop. Amelia does not mention the vandalism. Instead, she starts talking about her boss. "Leo Tessier is not a bad person," she says, "but when it comes to food, he is living in the past. He pays no attention to trends or to the environment. If you ask me, it's irresponsible." I can hear Stacey going,

"Hmm" in the background. "People," Amelia continues, "especially young people, want more vegetarian options these days—and it's not only a matter of taste. They want to eat sustainably and responsibly. If I ever get to be head chef at this cafeteria, the first thing I'm going to do is take his *rôti de boeuf* and *sole amandine* off the menu and replace them with soybean burgers and lentil loaf. That's what people want, and that's what our planet needs!"

Stacey claps.

"Why are you clapping?" Nico asks. "This whole thing is fake."

"I'm not so sure about that," Stacey tells him. "Besides, even if it is, it's very inspiring!"

There is still one more potential suspect on the video. This one is a young guy around Lloyd and Samantha's age. He is wearing a Che Guevara T-shirt and a black beret like Che's. The bottom of the screen says *Jonah Cartwright, student*. "I don't know why anyone would think I vandalized the cafeteria," he says, shrugging his shoulders. "I have way too much schoolwork to do something dumb like that. But I want to be up front with you: it is true that I have been involved in a number of important student strikes. But those were different. We were protesting possible tuition hikes. Look, I'll even admit that the police picked me up one night for defacing university property—but that was two years ago. I'm through with that kind of stuff. I swear I am."

The same woman's voice we heard before asks Jonah whether he eats meat and fish.

"Absolutely not!" Jonah sounds insulted, "I'm vegan."

The woman asks whether Jonah has any problem with other people eating meat and fish and whether he thinks the university cafeteria should have more vegetarian options.

"Now that you mention it," Jonah says, "more vegetarian and vegan options would be cool."

"I hope you guys took notes," Lloyd tells us when the video is over.

Stacey looks up. "I made a list of everything they said."

"You've just met your four suspects," Samantha tells us. "I think you'll agree that each one has a plausible motive for vandalizing the cafeteria."

Lloyd needs Samantha's help to get supplies for our next activity, and so for a few minutes it is just the six of us at the conference table.

Nico does a double swivel in his chair. "I still think Mrs. Lu did it."

"Even if she feels frustrated, I don't think Mrs. Lu would risk losing her job. Not when she has a family to support," I say.

Mason grins at me from across the table. "Now who's talking about forensics camp as if it's real?"

NINE

When the counselors get back, they are each carrying a long tub with sand in it. Lloyd arranges the two tubs side by side on the floor. "Most people don't realize how much information footwear evidence can provide. I need two volunteers for our next activity. How 'bout Mason and Tabitha?"

"Sure!" I say. I want to learn everything I can about footwear evidence. And not just because no one took footwear impressions at the scene of our break-and-enter.

Lloyd asks us to walk on the sand. "Just the way you'd normally walk. Without thinking about it."

Mason and I walk through the sand, and then we all gather to examine the evidence.

We can see right away that my feet are smaller than Mason's, but Lloyd also shows us how the tracks in the sand reveal that Mason is wearing runners and I have sandals on.

"What else do you see?" Lloyd watches for our reactions. He obviously takes being FIG seriously.

Nico raises his hand. "I see two tubs of sand!"

Lloyd ignores Nico. "I want you guys to think about the different ways people walk. A person's walk is kind of like their signature. For example, I've noticed that Tabitha walks quickly, with her chin leading the way."

I do? That's news to me. I pat my chin. Maybe observing other people is easier than observing ourselves.

"Now, Mason takes his time when he walks."

That, on the other hand, is definitely not news. How many hours of my life have I spent waiting for Mason to catch up to me? "I want you to look carefully. Can you find evidence of those habits in their footwear impressions?"

When Lloyd asks that question, it's like a lightbulb goes on over my head—just like in a cartoon. When I look at my footwear impressions, I see the indentations are deeper at the toe than at the sole. Mason's indentations are more even. How cool is that!

"There's more," Lloyd says. "Every shoe has unique wear indentations." He points to a fan-shaped spot at the bottom of my left impression. "I'd say the heel of Tabatha's left sandal is coming loose." I kick off the sandal and turn it over. Lloyd is right. I am going to have to take my sandals to the shoe-repair guy.

Nathaniel leans over to get a closer look at the bottom of my sandal. "Wow!" he says.

Lloyd tugs on the bottom of his earlobe. "I must be hearing things—because I thought I heard Nathaniel use the word *wow*," he says.

Samantha has been taking photographs of both sets of footwear impressions and uploading the files to a computer, but I know she is listening to Lloyd's lesson. "Hey, we don't call him FIG for nothing," she says.

"That's right," Lloyd says. "Other things you can look for include materials that can get trapped on the sole of a shoe. For example, nails or wadded-up chewing gum," he explains.

Nathaniel nods. "I once heard my dad say that one of the first thing cops do when they stop a suspect is make them hand over their shoes. Now I know why."

"Exactly," Lloyd says. "You don't want to give a suspect time to change his or her shoes."

Samantha has projected the images of our footwear impressions onto the screen. "Let's zoom in for a closer look," she tells us.

Samantha clicks past one or two blurry images, stopping when she gets to a sharp photograph of Mason's footwear impressions. "Look carefully," she says. "What do you see?"

"The Nike swish. I mean swash. I mean swoosh!" Nico calls out.

Muriel gives him a whack. "That's not even a little bit funny," she tells him, and Nico makes a pouty face.

"Nico's right about the swoosh though," Lloyd says. "We can match Mason's footwear impressions with the information in our database—and then we should be able to determine exactly which model of Nikes he was wearing. Footwear impressions can also reveal a person's shoe size."

Stacey clicks her Department of Forensic Science pen. "Does that mean we can identify someone from their footwear impressions the way we can from their fingerprints?" she asks.

"No way," Nathaniel says. "Shoes aren't one of a kind."

"That's right," Lloyd says. "Think of the thousands of pairs of runners Nike sells every year. Footwear impressions are not what we call individualizing, the way fingerprints are. Hey, have you guys ever heard of Theodore Kaczynski?"

I start to raise my hand, but then I stop myself. I have to remember that this is camp, not school. "You mean the Unabomber?" I say. "The guy who produced sixteen bombs, which injured twenty-three people and killed three others?" The *Junior Encyclopedia of Forensic Science* has a long entry about Theodore Kaczynski.

"Exactly. Kaczynski attached smaller soles to the bottom of his shoes as a way to confuse investigators," Lloyd tells us.

Nathaniel nods. That makes twice in one day that Nathaniel has been impressed.

TEN

It is a short walk to the university's athletic complex. The air is so hot and humid, it's hard to imagine there could ever be winter in Montreal. Even though we are walking on the shady side of the street, under a canopy of maple trees, I feel the sweat trickling down my back and making my T-shirt sticky. I can't wait to jump into the swimming pool.

"I don't need swimming lessons," I hear Nathaniel tell Mason. "I've been swimming since I was six months old, and I've already passed Red Cross Level 10. I can do every stroke."

"Even the butterfly?" Mason asks. "I can't do the butterfly. To be honest, I'm not the greatest swimmer."

"The butterfly's not that hard," Nathaniel tells him, "once you get the kick."

We are wearing our bathing suits under our regular clothes, so it doesn't take long to change. I can smell the chlorine—even from inside the change room.

"I was hoping they'd have a saltwater pool," Stacey says. "In its artificial form, chlorine depletes the ozone layer and contributes to global warming. I'm going to start a list of things the university could do to green this campus."

Stacey and I are barefoot. Muriel's flip-flops slap against the tile deck. The counselors are waiting outside the locker rooms. Lloyd has a whistle hanging from a rope around his neck. Samantha is carrying a clipboard. How did she tuck all that hair into a bathing cap?

Of course, Mason is the last one out. He is humming the way he sometimes does when he gets nervous. His Batman towel is wrapped loosely around his waist.

Lloyd squats down in front of us like he's a football coach and we're his team. "I bet you've heard that applicants to police academy have to be in top physical form. Well, the same goes for forensic scientists. That's why exercise is an important part of this camp. Swimming is great for all-around conditioning. I don't tell this to a lot of people,"— Lloyd lowers his voice like he is letting us in on a state secret—"but I used to be well...chubby. Okay, more than chubby. Swimming helped me slim down and get strong."

Nathaniel nudges Mason. "Hey dude, maybe a little swimming'll do the trick for you too."

Mason blushes. Not just his face, but even his chest gets a little red.

Why does Nathaniel have to be such a jerk? I shoot him a look and mouth the words *Shut up*. I do not want Mason to know I'm standing up for him.

Nathaniel shrugs. Still, I think he got the message. Just in case, I narrow my eyes at him.

Nathaniel gives Mason another nudge. "I was just kidding," he says.

Lloyd has not intervened. Probably because he wants to let us sort things out ourselves. Work as a team. "All right then," Lloyd says, clapping his hands. "This afternoon, we'll review some basics, then you're going to do some laps so Samantha and I can assess your fitness levels."

Nathaniel does a perfect racing dive into the deep end. Talk about showing off! The rest of us jump in. The water feels so fresh and cool that Muriel and I scream with pleasure. Mason is the last one in.

Lloyd and Samantha wave us over to the side. "We'll start with a simple exercise. I want you each to take a deep breath"—Lloyd demonstrates by resting his hands on his belly as he inhales—"and now hold your breath and cross your legs. Watch what happens next."

Because I'm expecting to sink, I scrunch up my eyes and pinch my nose. Except I don't sink. I'm not even treading, just holding my breath and keeping my legs crossed the way Lloyd told us to. The others are not sinking either. Only Stacey is struggling. For a moment, all I see is the top of her head. Then even that disappears under the water until she comes up again, sputtering and shaking her head like a wet dog.

Lloyd squats down on the pool ledge. "Ninety-five percent of people are buoyant." He looks over at Stacey. "Unfortunately," he tells her, "it looks like you're in the other five percent.

What this exercise proves—for the rest of you anyhow—is you don't have to work that hard to stay afloat. Why don't you try treading now—slow and easy so you conserve energy."

Nathaniel and Nico are starting to puff. Next to them, Mason is breathing comfortably. He is doing just what Lloyd said—treading water slow and easy.

"Most people don't realize this," Lloyd says, "but when you're in water, a little extra weight can actually be an advantage. It makes you more buoyant. Skinny, muscular kids? They're the first to sink."

After we've treaded for five minutes, Lloyd asks us each to take a lane and demonstrate our front crawl. Samantha walks the length of the pool, jotting notes on her clipboard. I wonder what they are going to do with all the info, but I still try my best to beat Muriel and Nico.

Afterward, Lloyd and Samantha have comments for everyone, even Nathaniel. Lloyd tells Muriel and me that we should not be scooping water with our hands. "Your hands should be sliding through the water—palms flat and turned sideways."

"You're lifting your head every time you breathe," Samantha tells Mason. "That creates unnecessary drag. Once we get that fixed, you'll pick up speed."

We get the last fifteen minutes to practice or just fool around in the water. Lloyd throws a striped beach ball into the pool, and the boys toss it around.

Stacey treads water. Muriel and I go to the shallow end to practice moving our hands through the water without cupping them.

When camp is over at four o'clock and Mason and I are on our way home, we notice that Nathaniel is headed in our direction. It turns out he lives in the same neighborhood we do, and so the three of us walk home together.

"How come we never saw you around before?" I ask Nathaniel.

"We only moved here two years ago. After Grandpa got sick, we needed a bigger place—so my grandparents could move in with us."

"Does your grandmother still live with you?" Mason asks.

"Yup—and now *he* does too." *He* must be his grandma's fiancé.

I'd like to know more, but Mason changes the subject. "What school do you go to?"

"Trudeau Academy," Nathaniel answers. Trudeau Academy is a private all-boys school with a reputation for being super strict.

"I guess that explains why we never met before," Mason says. "I'm glad your parents signed you up for forensics camp."

Nathaniel whacks Mason with his backpack. "I'm glad you're glad." To my surprise, there is nothing sarcastic in Nathaniel's tone.

Unfortunately, the sidewalk is not very wide, and I end up having to walk behind the two of them. They are talking about the Unabomber and the butterfly stroke.

"I'm not bad at the butterfly," I say, but they don't hear me over the sound of the rush-hour traffic. When I turn to look into the street, I see a row of cars and two city buses full of passengers. No one is paying any attention to a small gray hatchback stalled at the side of the road. Right now I feel a little like that hatchback.

That is the moment when I realize that after thirteen years of being stuck with Mason, he is finally making a new friend—just like I told him he should. So why do I feel like an abandoned vehicle? And how come I'm not happy for Mason?

We come to Nathaniel's house first. It is brick with a copper roof that has turned green. A pink rosebush in full bloom climbs the front railing. An elegant-looking woman with shoulder-length gray hair stands in the front window. She is holding a small dog who is wagging his tail. When the woman waves at us, the dog jumps out of her arms, and I can see the woman laugh. She laughs with her whole face— her eyes, her cheeks, not just her mouth.

"Is that your grandmother?" I ask Nathaniel.

"Yup, that's her. At least *he*'s not there too."

"Is that your dog?" Mason asks.

"Actually, it's my grandpa's—" Nathaniel stops himself. "I mean, my grandma's dog. Willy's a Pomeranian. He used to dance a circle around my grandpa every day when he got back from work. And after Grandpa got sick, Willy hardly ever left his side." Nathaniel's voice softens; he doesn't sound as if he is trying to be a big shot when he remembers his grandpa.

An older man with a bald head and wire glasses comes to join Nathaniel's grandmother in the window. He looks okay to me.

"That's *him*."

There is nothing soft about the way Nathaniel says it.

ELEVEN

That night, as I am putting away the cutlery in the cutlery drawer and Dad is inspecting the floor for crumbs, Mom says, "If you two don't mind, I'd like to do another hour or so of paperwork."

Dad strokes her arm. "No problem."

"Working is good for her," I say to Dad when Mom leaves the room. It seems like an obvious observation, but somehow I never thought of it before. "It's the relaxing she has trouble with."

Dad sighs. "I think it's when she's relaxing—or trying to relax—that the anxious thoughts come back. That's why I'm hoping the meditation will help. Are you sure you don't want to try it with us, Tab?"

"I've already got my own way to relax."

Dad drops the crumbs he has scooped up into the garbage. He points a finger at me. "Let me guess. It has something to do with reading up about forensics, right?"

I high-five Dad. "You know what? For a numbers guy, you're pretty smart about people."

Dad grins. Then he grabs a dishcloth from the counter. He has noticed a smudge on the refrigerator door. "Sometimes I wonder…" Dad leaves the words dangling in midair.

"What do you wonder sometimes?" I prompt him.

"Nah, nothing," he says, wiping away the smudge.

Now I'm curious. "C'mon, Dad, tell me."

He folds the dishcloth into two and hangs it over the faucet. "Well, sometimes I wonder how much you remember about the break-and-enter. I know you didn't see anything. But maybe it had more of an effect on you than we realized." His voice is quieter than usual. Probably because he does not want Mom to overhear us. Or he's worried about upsetting me.

"All I remember are bits and pieces," I tell him. Without planning to, I have lowered my voice too. "How I went upstairs to color. It's weird, but I even remember the smell of the crayons. When I heard noises from downstairs, I thought Mom had turned on the TV, though I remember thinking she didn't usually like noisy shows. I covered my ears when the noises got louder. Then nothing else until the policeman came to get me…" Only now, something else is coming back to me. Something I never remembered before. Another smell. Something sour. Pee. Why pee? "Dad…did I pee myself during the break-in?"

"Uh-huh," Dad says gently. "The police officer found you standing in a puddle of pee—with your hands over your ears."

"How come we never talk about it?" I ask.

"Your mom and I always thought you'd talk about it if you wanted to. We didn't want to push you. And to be honest, your mom was such a mess after the whole thing happened, well, the focus was mostly on her. You seemed to be able to move right past it."

Dad strokes my cheek. I don't even realize I am crying until he wipes the tears away. "I'm so sorry we didn't handle it better…"

"It's okay, Dad." When I reach to touch his cheek, I realize it's damp too.

We don't say anything else as we put away the dishes and shut off the kitchen lights, but it's a good kind of quiet.

Afterward I go to the den to read the *Junior Encyclopedia of Forensic Science*. I could read in my room, but I'm not in the mood to be alone right now, and I figure Dad will probably end up in the den too. Besides, I feel like hanging out with him some more—even if we don't end up talking.

The den still smells like incense, but there is no sign of the candle. I am reading about methods for detecting poison in corpses when Dad comes in with his laptop. "Tab, I was hoping you'd want to help me to do some research"—his voice is flat, so I am not expecting much, until he adds— "about where a person might buy a German shepherd. I hear they make excellent guard dogs."

"Dad!" I pop up from the couch. When the *Junior Encyclopedia of Forensic Science*, my favorite book in all the world, falls to the carpet, I leave it lying there. I throw my arms around my dad and then we sit on the couch next to each other.

"I promise I'll clean up every single strand of dog hair," I tell Dad. "And every pile of poop."

Dad strokes my elbow. "You know, Tabitha, over the years your mom's talked about getting a dog or a cat. She thought that after everything you'd been through, and since you were an only child, a pet would be good for you. I'm the one who always said no, mostly because I didn't want to deal with the mess. Maybe it's time I loosened up a little."

"Let me guess," I tell him. "You figured that out when you were meditating."

I can tell Dad is trying not to smile. "Maybe."

Dad's laptop is open, and I can see he has googled *German shepherds + breeders + Montreal area*. I am almost too excited to think straight!

"It looks like most of the breeders are outside of the city," Dad says as he scans the screen. "We might be able to go on the weekend."

"What about this one?" I point to a listing that says *Kijiji—amazing deals on purebred dogs of all kinds, Montreal.*

A lot of people use Kijiji, a free online classified-ads service. Maybe the purebreds the site is advertising include German shepherds.

Dad moves the cursor so it hovers over the listing, but he doesn't click on it. "I don't like the idea of buying a dog on Kijiji," he says. "Winter tires or a washing machine maybe. But not a dog. I'm more comfortable dealing with a breeder. Even if it ends up costing more."

Dad scrolls down the page.

"Hey, what about that one?" I say. I've spotted a listing for German shepherd puppies. "Can you imagine how cute a German shepherd puppy would be?"

"Cute, yes, but I don't think a puppy is the way to go," Dad says. "For one thing, puppies are a ton of work. We'd have to paper-train him—"

"Or her."

"Or her. I think I'm ready to deal with dog hair. But poop and pee in the house? I'd need to meditate a lot more before I could handle that. Besides, if we really want to go ahead and train him—or her—to be a guard dog, that'd be even more work, not to mention time."

I have an idea. "What if we search for an already-trained German shepherd guard dog and see what happens? It's worth a try."

Because Dad knows I am even faster on the keyboard than he is, he passes the laptop over to me.

The first listing is for what someone is calling a senior German shepherd. Apparently the dog has a great personality, but he is having some trouble with his hind legs.

Dad clicks on the dog's picture. "Poor fellow," he says. "But I guess full range of movement is a must for a guard dog."

There's another listing for a German shepherd guard dog that someone wants to give away for free. Only this one isn't good around kids. "I bet that's code for he bites," Dad says.

"Can you imagine Mom around a dog who bites? She'd have a heart attack every time he opened his mouth."

Dad is already reading the next listing. "Hey, have a look at this one," he says

I am already having a look. *Montreal dog trainer looking to sell recently retired guard dog. Price is negotiable. What matters most is finding the right home.* I click on the link for more details. It takes us to the dog trainer's website. He specializes in training guard dogs. He has a seven-year-old German shepherd who recently retired from the guard-dog business but is in good shape. "We need to make sure he's still capable of guarding a house," Dad says. "And that he's healthy…and only bites bad guys, not kids."

"Seven is forty-nine in dog years," I tell Dad. "That isn't old."

Dad chuckles—he is forty-nine too.

I click on the *Contact me* bar, and together Dad and I compose a message. *We are interested in the guard dog you have for sale. Is he still in good enough shape to guard a house? If so, we're wondering if we could meet him.*

I hit *Send.*

"You never know," Dad is saying when the computer pings a few minutes later.

Roxie is in excellent shape and would make a fine family guard dog. I really wish I could keep her, but my place isn't big, and I've already got two dogs. What matters most to me is that she goes to the right home. You can meet Roxie pretty much any time. Let me know when would work for you. I'm on Sherbrooke Street West.

Sherbrooke Street West? That's not far from where we live. Dad must be thinking the same thing. I catch him checking the time at the top of the computer screen—4:45 PM. "Why don't we write back and ask if we can go meet Roxie now?" he says.

After we set things up with the trainer—his name is Larry—Dad calls out to Mom, "Lila, Tabitha and I are going to go for a little drive. D'you want us to pick up anything while we're out?"

"No, but thanks for asking," Mom calls back. She must still be hard at work. Otherwise, she'd come to the door to say goodbye. Just as we are in the hallway putting on our shoes, she calls, "Don't forget to reset the alarm when you go!"

The barking starts before Dad and I are out of the car. When Larry comes to the door, there are three German shepherds at his heels. One of them is muzzled and making a low growl. I hope that isn't Roxie.

"Everything's good," Larry says, and as if on cue, the dogs settle down, even the one wearing the muzzle. I wonder if the dogs have been trained to respond to the words *Everything's good*.

Another dog is wagging his—or is it her?—tail. The dog has one ear that sticks up and another that flops over. I hope that's Roxie.

"Come right in." I can feel Larry studying us. We are here to see if we like Roxie, but now I realize Larry is deciding whether he likes us.

"I'm Rob Letour," my dad says. "And this is my daughter, Tabitha. If you don't mind my asking, why is that dog muzzled?"

"Pixie's a fear biter," Larry explains. "She bites when she's anxious. A lot of dogs who bite are fear biters. There are people like that too—the kind who snap because they're scared."

I'm just glad the muzzled dog isn't Roxie. "Nice to meet you," I say, reaching out to shake Larry's hand firmly. I want to impress him with my good manners. "Is that one Roxie?" I ask about the dog with the funny ears.

"That's Roxie, all right. I got her when she was a pup and trained her to be a guard dog. She was a natural— curious and alert. I rent my guard dogs out. Roxie worked at a car dealership. The people over there would have kept her longer, but I have a policy of retiring my dogs after they've worked six years." Roxie has come to sit down on her hind legs next to Larry. He leans down to scratch her forehead. "This girl deserves some downtime."

Roxie's funny ears are pricked in a way that makes me think she knows we are talking about her.

Larry turns to us. "Why don't you tell me a little about yourselves?"

My dad goes first. "Tabitha here came up with the idea of getting a guard dog. We had a break-in a few years back." Dad looks over at me as if he is asking my permission to go on with the story. I nod to tell him it is okay. "Tabitha and my wife were both home at the time," he adds. "Luckily, Tabitha was in her room upstairs, so she didn't see the thieves. Which may be why she bounced back afterward. But my wife, well, she witnessed the crime and she's been a bit"—Dad is trying to come up with the right word— "uneasy ever since. We've tried everything—alarm system, meditation, yoga, therapy—so when Tabitha suggested getting a dog, I thought it was a good idea."

I can see Larry watching my dad, noticing how he cracks his knuckles when he talks about my mom. "It sounds like what you're looking for is more a working dog than a family dog," Larry says.

If I don't say something, he may not let us have Roxie. "We're looking for a working dog who can be part of our family." I can't help smiling when I say that. The sentence came out even better than I planned. "Roxie's a beautiful dog. I promise that if you let us have her, we'll take really good care of her."

I know it's a good sign when Larry and Dad start discussing money. Larry does not want much for Roxie. "But I've got some conditions I'd like you to agree to before I consider letting you have her," he tells us. Roxie is used to a lot of physical activity, so she will need to be taken for walks at least twice a day. He is adamant about that, and I promise to take Roxie out every day, rain or shine.

"We have a big backyard where she can run around too," I tell Larry. Then I look at Roxie. "Wait till you see the yard. You'll love it."

Larry also says Roxie needs to be fed a special raw-food diet, and he'd like her to continue to see her regular veterinarian for checkups.

"None of that's a problem," Dad says. "I'd like to bring my wi—"

Larry talks over my dad. "Before I decide anything, I want to meet your wi—"

For a second their faces freeze, and then Dad and Larry both start laughing.

"Can we go and get her right now?" I ask Dad.

We text Mom first to tell her to be ready. She is standing by the door when we pull up in front of the house. I hop out and get into the backseat. "Wait till you see Roxie," I tell her. "You're gonna love her."

"Is it my imagination," Mom says, "or does all this seem to be happening very quickly?"

"It feels like kismet," Dad tells her.

"What's kismet?" I ask. If Nico were here, he'd make some crack about kissing.

"Kismet is fate," Dad says. "Like all of this was meant to be."

Mom catches his eye. "All of it?" she asks. Why do I get the feeling they are talking about something I cannot understand?

"Yup," he says, reaching over to pat the back of her hand. "All of it."

I hate to interrupt a tender moment, but I have to. "Mom, don't act too weird around the trainer."

Mom turns around to look at me. "Me? Act weird?"

I am relieved when we get back to Larry's place and Mom does not bring up the robbery. "Her coat looks shiny," Mom says, petting Roxie. "Do you suppose that's because of her diet, Larry?"

"Absolutely." Then Larry looks hard at my mom. "I heard there was a break-in at your place a while back. That you were pretty traumatized afterward."

"Oh, that was years ago." Mom's voice is lighter and more casual than usual, so I know she's putting on an act.

"Roxie's a fine guard dog," Larry says, "but if you don't mind my saying, I've had some experience with people like you—people whose homes have been broken into. People who've been victimized."

"What are you trying to say exactly?" Mom asks.

"I'm saying no one else—not even a guard dog—can make it better. That's got to come from in here." He taps the side of his head.

I'm starting to worry. Mom hates when people offer advice about her anxiety. What if she snaps at Larry?

Mom asks Roxie to sit down and give her a paw. She laughs when Roxie responds immediately. Then Mom looks up at Larry. "Thanks," she says to him.

That's when Larry agrees to let us have Roxie. Mom writes him a check. Before we go, Larry demonstrates how Roxie responds to simple commands like "heel," "down" and "stay." He watches while I try out the commands. "Make sure to use a firm voice. Like I just did," Larry says. He smiles a little wistfully when Roxie heels, lies down and stays. It turns out I was right about the words *Everything's good*. They are Roxie's cue to relax.

"What's the cue to get Roxie to attack?" I ask Larry.

At first Larry does not answer. He just looks at me and shakes his head. "You don't need to know stuff like that, Tabitha. When a dog like Roxie goes on the attack, things get ugly."

"But what if we need Roxie to protect us?"

I can tell Larry is thinking about my question. "There's one cue I'll let you use—but don't play around with it." Larry gestures for me to follow him a few steps away, so Roxie won't hear what he is about to say. "Knee him," he whispers.

"Knee him?" I whisper back.

"Yup. That Roxie's cue to knock someone over. Not make him bleed, just knock him—or her—over. There's a hand signal too."

"A hand signal?"

"Absolutely," Larry says. "That's in case someone is trying to prevent you from speaking." Larry puts his hands over his mouth to demonstrate.

"Yikes." Even thinking about that makes me nervous.

After Larry shows me the hand signal, we walk back to join my parents and Roxie. "You'll need to work with Roxie. Practice the commands I taught Tabitha. You'll find Roxie enjoys it," Larry tells us, but I notice he is mostly talking to me. He must understand that Roxie is going to be *my* dog.

At 7:15 PM—or 19:15 hours in forensic-science-speak—we prepare to leave with the newest member of our family, Roxie.

Larry goes back into the house for Roxie's dog bed and her favorite toy, a rubber stick. Then he walks us to our car. Pixie, the fear biter, is supervising from the porch.

"If you don't mind," Larry says, "I'd like a minute alone with Roxie. To say goodbye."

I cannot hear what Larry is saying, but I can tell it is not easy for him to let Roxie go.

"There's one more thing," he tells us before we pile into the car. "I don't know whether or not you've heard, but a number of dogs in the Montreal area—all purebreds—have gone missing in the last couple of weeks. And I also heard on the grapevine that a box of bark breakers were stolen from a pet store downtown."

"Bark breakers?" Mom asks.

"They're collars that release citronella spray every time a dog barks. One stolen collar wouldn't concern me, but when I heard a whole box went missing, well, I got to wondering…"

I suddenly remember the posters I have seen—the missing Chihuahua and then the standard poodle. Both purebreds. I assumed the dogs had run away, but maybe it's something more sinister.

"Are you suggesting they might have been *dog*napped?" I ask Larry.

"All I'm suggesting is it's suspicious," he answers.

On the drive home, Roxie sits next to me in the backseat. She turns to look at Larry, who is standing in his driveway, waving. She barks when we turn the corner and Larry is out of view. "We're gonna take good care of you, girl," I promise her. I don't have a lot of experience looking after someone else—but I feel ready for the responsibility.

Roxie spreads out on the backseat and lays her head in my lap. Mom reaches from the front seat to pat Roxie's head.

TWELVE

This morning when I reached into the top drawer of my nightstand, I happened to grab my ransom-note bracelet. It's a leather cord with wooden alphabet beads, each a different color and printed in a different font. It spells out *LEAVE THE CASH IN AN UNMARKED ENVELOPE.*

"That's the perfect bracelet for today, Tabitha," Lloyd says when he notices it. "Day three at forensics camp starts with a lesson in document analysis."

Samantha does not do chitchat the way Lloyd does. Once she's through taking attendance, she tells us to take out our notebooks. "Forensic scientists use document analysis to examine evidence such as ransom notes, forgeries and threatening letters," she says.

"Yeah, but how's any of that going to help us figure out who trashed the cafeteria?" Nathaniel calls out.

"I'll get to that, Nathaniel," Samantha tells him.

"What about the mustard message?" I wonder out loud. "Couldn't that be considered a document—sort of?"

"Possibly," is all Samantha will say.

Except for her purple glasses, Samantha looks even more businesslike than usual today. She is wearing a white shirt and a plain gray skirt. I wonder if she even owns a pair of jeans. "We're going to begin by looking at something called imprints," she tells us. "Do any of you know what an imprint is?"

The others look at me. Ever since I answered the question about Theodore Kaczynski, they expect me to know everything. On the one hand, I'm honored. On the other hand, it makes me feel pressured. Especially when I don't know the answer, like now. So I shrug and try to look like I don't care, even though I do.

"Instead of boring you with the definition, I'm going to show you what an imprint looks like. Stacey, if you could pass me your notebook, please." Samantha opens the notebook to the last page Stacey wrote on. "I don't know if the rest of you have noticed, but Stacey presses down really hard when she writes. Which is why I asked for her notebook. Now have a look at this." Samantha turns the page. "Do you see anything?"

We pass the notebook around. When Nathaniel holds it up to the fluorescent light, we can see pale scratches from where Stacey pressed down, but we cannot make out any letters or words.

Lloyd brings a small square box from the supply cupboard. Inside are two flashlights. One looks like a regular flashlight, except it has three settings: normal, white light and infrared. The other is a small rectangular ultra-violet light. We start with the regular flashlight, holding it so the light is shining directly on Stacey's notebook, but we still can't make out the letters. Not until we move the flashlight so the light is coming from the side. Now there's a shadow, which lets us see the imprint of Stacey's handwriting: *ransom notes, forgeries and threatening letters.*

Wow! So if a kidnapper wrote a ransom note on a pad of paper and tore the note off the pad, the police might be able to find the imprint!

Stacey is thinking about something else. "Too bad mustard doesn't leave an imprint," she says.

"You're right about mustard," Lloyd says, "but forensic graphologists—the term for forensic scientists who specialize in document analysis—can do other things with handwriting. Even mustard handwriting. You guys ready to learn a little more?"

We all nod. Forensics camp keeps getting more and more interesting. If only we learned stuff like this at school!

"Forensic graphologists look at similarities and differences in handwriting. They study characteristics such as spacing between letters or lines, slants, patterns in letters and loops on certain letters. Did you guys write all that down?"

"Almost," Muriel says without looking up from her notebook.

"Perfect! Because we're going to study samples of your handwriting. Nico, let's start by having a look at yours." Lloyd gestures for us to come over so we can all examine

Nico's handwriting. "Do you see any identifying characteristics? Think about some of the things I just asked you to
write down."

"It's messy," Muriel says. "Does that count as an identifying characteristic?"

"Not really," Lloyd says. "Can you try to be a little more
specific?"

"Well, his letters are really crowded together," Muriel says.

"That's better. Now you're talking about spacing."

"He didn't dot his *i*'s," I say, pointing to the words
forensic and *similarities*.

"That's only because I was rushing," Nico says.

Stacey shakes her head. "You're always rushing."

"And making bad jokes," Muriel adds.

We look at all of our handwriting. Of the six of us,
Muriel leaves the most space between her letters. Stacey's
handwriting is the smallest. Mason's is the straightest, and
the lines across Nathaniel's small *t*'s are lower down than the
rest of ours. I don't always bother dotting my *i*'s. "Those are
all excellent observations," Lloyd says. "I think you're ready
to learn a new trick."

He reaches back into the square box and takes out a pad
of tracing paper and a bundle of pencils. Then he borrows
Nico's notebook again to demonstrate what he wants us to
do next. Lloyd puts a piece of tracing paper over the longest
line Nico has written, and then he makes a dot at the highest
point that every letter reaches. "Now I connect the dots
horizontally," he says. The line Lloyd gets by connecting the
dots reminds me of a mountain range in the Himalayas.

"This line shows us the top slope of Nico's handwriting. Even if a person is in a rush and doesn't have time to dot his *i*'s, handwriting slope tends to be consistent. We're going to do the same thing with the bottom slope."

"That means we should be able to examine the slope of the mustard handwriting!" Nathaniel says.

"We should," Samantha says, "*if* the photos you and Mason took are sharp enough."

"We've got one more exercise to do first though," Lloyd says. Samantha hands him an envelope from the square box. Inside are three bundles of bank checks. "You'll be working with your partners for this activity," Lloyd continues. He gives each group a check from each of the bundles. "You will notice that all of these checks are in the amount of one thousand dollars. Each check is signed by someone named Edgar Rich. Two of the checks in your bundle were actually signed by Mr. Rich. Your task is to uncover the forgery."

"Rich is the right name for this dude," Nico says. "Imagine writing nine thousand bucks' worth of checks!"

Muriel sighs. "Did you look at the date, Nico? The year says 1952. I'm pretty sure they're expired by now."

At first glance, all three Edgar Rich signatures look identical. "Wouldn't a professional forger be able to copy someone's slope and get the little details right—like how a person dots his letters and crosses his *t*'s?" Stacey asks.

"That's true," Lloyd says. "Professional forgers know about all the things we've covered this morning. But it's virtually impossible to get someone else's signature exactly right.

That's because a signature doesn't just come from someone's hand—it comes from their brain."

We are all thinking about that when Muriel says, "I knew how to forge my fifth-grade teacher's signature." Then she adds as an afterthought, "Don't worry—I never did it. I just knew how."

Maybe it's because Muriel has a background in forging teachers' signatures that she notices the tiny extra squiggle at the bottom of one of the *g*'s in the *Edgar*. We decide that check is probably the forgery, but we want to confirm our hunch. Muriel traces the top slope on all three signatures; I trace the bottom. When it turns out the top slope is less jagged on the check with the squiggly *g*, we raise our hands so that we can show the counselors what we have found. Lloyd says we have done such a good job that we should go and help the others.

"Can we please, *please* start analyzing the mustard message?" Muriel asks.

Samantha claps to get everyone's attention. "I know you're all anxious to apply your new graphology skills to the mustard message. And you will be doing that today. But first"—she pauses, and I can tell it's because she thinks we are going to get excited about what she is about to say— "there's the obstacle course."

"You mean the sort of obstacle course you have to do before you can get accepted into police academy?" Nico asks. For once, he is not trying to make a joke.

"You got it," Lloyd says.

Someone in the room makes a gagging sound.

"Mason?" Samantha says. "Is something wrong?"

"Uh, I'm just feeling a little queasy. Maybe there was something wrong with the milk in my cereal this morning." He does not say he feels too queasy to do the obstacle course. But I have known Mason Johnson long enough to know that is exactly what he is thinking.

THIRTEEN

It is hard to believe Lloyd was ever out of shape. Especially when he demonstrates how to do the obstacle course.

He has set things up behind the Life Sciences Building, where there is a large concrete terrace and two sets of stairs leading to a rooftop vegetable garden. It is a quiet spot, so we are not likely to get in anyone's way.

Stacey approves of the garden's rainwater collection system. "That's for harvesting rain," she says, pointing to a giant barrel. It seems weird to use the words *harvesting* and *rain* together, but there isn't time to discuss that with Stacey, even if I wanted to.

Lloyd is doing ten push-ups on the terrace. His back is stick straight, and his elbows are slightly bent. When he is done, Samantha tosses him a red medicine ball ("Those things are a lot heavier than they look," Nathaniel says), and Lloyd runs up and down the stairs—twice. Next he bounces the medicine ball, slamming it against the concrete five times before catching it again and dashing to the next station. The guy has not even broken a sweat.

Nathaniel nudges Mason. "How's your stomach?"

"Not so good." Mason looks pale. Maybe it is from the thought of having to do ten push-ups.

Next Lloyd crawls through two narrow, ten-foot coiled tubes that are set up on the terrace.

We can see the outline of Lloyd's elbows as he pushes his way through the tubes. "That looks really hard," Stacey says.

"You think that's hard? Wait till you see him jump over the wall!" Samantha tells her.

"Jump over a wall?" Mason gulps. "You're joking, right?"

"Do I strike you as the joking type?" Samantha asks. "But hey, don't worry—the wall here is only four feet high. You'd have to jump a lot higher than that to get into the police academy."

The wall is actually a concrete divider at the shady end of the terrace. "I want you to watch Lloyd's technique," Samantha tells us. "He's going to use his upper body strength to lift himself up and over."

We all watch as Lloyd places both hands on top of the wall, a foot or so apart. He hoists one leg up, then the other. He seems totally calm and focused. But when he swings his legs over the wall and drops to the other side, he makes this wild whooping sound, and we clap and cheer for him.

"Don't think this obstacle course is over yet!" Lloyd shouts back at us.

We follow Samantha under the stairway so we can catch up with Lloyd and see the final obstacle.

"Oh my god," I say when I see what is lying on the concrete: a life-sized rubber dummy. Why are its wrists wrapped in duct tape? I figure out the answer when Lloyd, who has finally started to sweat, grabs the dummy by its wrists and starts dragging it over the concrete. I guess the duct tape gives him something to grip.

"Do you see how he's bending his knees?" Samantha says. "That's because he's letting his legs do most of the work." Lloyd's calf muscles are twitching.

When he has dragged the dummy past a yellow chalk line on the concrete, Lloyd squats down and shakes out his arms. When he looks up at us, the sweat is pouring off his face. "You guys think you can do that?" he pants, still trying to catch his breath.

"No," Nico says, "but it's nice of you to ask."

Samantha checks her cell-phone stopwatch. "The obstacle course took Lloyd precisely two minutes and forty-two seconds."

Lloyd has stopped panting. "Any of you think you can beat that?" he asks.

Nathaniel straightens his shoulders. "Maybe."

Muriel eyes the dummy. "If you don't mind my asking, how much does that thing weigh?"

"One hundred and fifty pounds," Lloyd tells her. "Say you're a police officer and your partner falls unconscious. You have to be strong enough to drag him—or her—to safety."

Muriel shakes her head. "One hundred and fifty pounds? That's double what I weigh."

"You guys only have to drag the dummy as far as the chalk line—which is about three feet. If you ever do the police-training obstacle course, you'll have to drag him a lot farther than that."

"Are you doing the obstacle course too?" Stacey asks Samantha.

"I'm not dressed for it," Samantha says, pointing down at her gray skirt. "Otherwise I would. Definitely. What about you, Mason? You up for it, or are you still feeling queasy?"

Mason drops his eyes to the ground. "Yeah, I'm still kinda queasy..."

The counselors allow Mason to rest on a shady bench. They ask if he wants a bottle of water, but he says no.

Samantha uses the stopwatch on her cell phone to tell us each when to start. She is timing it so there will not be two of us at the same station. "Go!" she tells me, and I start doing the push-ups. I have never done ten in a row before, and when I get to six, I collapse on the ground.

"You can do it!" Samantha tells me, and I manage to complete the other four though I know my back is sagging.

Bouncing the medicine ball is harder than I expect. "You're doing great, Tabitha!" Lloyd calls out, only his voice sounds like it is coming from far away.

Nico is ahead of me. "Lemme out of here!" I hear him call from inside the first coil. "I'm getting claustrophobia!"

Which doesn't exactly make me look forward to that station. But when I get to the coils, it's not the narrowness inside that bothers me; it's the heat. The nylon coils have been baking all morning in the sun, and it is boiling inside them.

Somehow—don't ask me how—I manage to get over the wall on my first try. But I don't know how I'll ever pull that dummy. I tug with every ounce of my strength, but the monster refuses to budge. What's inside it? Lead? "Bend your knees!" Samantha hollers, but I am too tired even to do that.

"Bend your knees!" she shouts again, and when I do, the dummy begins to bump along the concrete. "Four minutes and thirty-seven seconds," Samantha says when I manage to get the dummy's head as far as the chalk line. "Maybe you'll be able to trim some time on your next go!"

My next go? I hope she's kidding!

But Lloyd has a different plan. "This time we're going to make two teams. And there'll be a prize at the end."

"What's the prize?" Nathaniel asks.

"I don't know," Lloyd says. "I haven't figured that out yet. What do you say—boys against the girls?"

"We can't make teams. Five's not an even number," Stacey points out.

"Shoot," Lloyd says, "I forgot about that."

Everyone is looking at Mason. Am I the only one who knows he's faking?

"Teams would've been cool," Nathaniel says in a loud voice.

When Mason gets up from the bench, I actually feel a little sorry for him. He hates team sports, probably because he is so bad at them. "Okay," he says, "I'm starting to feel a bit better. So I'll do it." He pauses for a second, then adds, "Just don't get mad if I mess up."

I know how hard this must be for Mason. But he is doing it. I have to admit I am ever-so-slightly impressed—not that I'd ever tell that to Mason.

Nathaniel punches Mason's arm, and Mason punches Nathaniel back.

"Come on, Tabitha!" Muriel yells.

"Let's show those boys!" Stacey adds.

Somehow, being part of a team makes the obstacle course less grueling.

I can hear Nathaniel and Nico cheering Mason on. From the corner of my eye, I can see him lumbering up the stairs with the medicine ball.

"Girls rule!" Muriel high-fives me when I finish.

Mason is trying for the third time to climb over the wall. "Use your upper body strength!" Lloyd reminds him. We all clap when he finally gets over. It is going to be painful to watch him trying to drag that dummy.

But Mason has no trouble with the dummy. He grabs hold of its wrists, and the dummy slides along the floor like it's filled with feathers.

Lloyd claps Mason's shoulder. "You're not fast," Lloyd says, "but man, are you ever strong. And that's on a day when your stomach is bothering you."

Mason isn't used to compliments. He throws back his shoulders. "To tell you the truth, I didn't even know I was strong," he says with a grin.

"Never underestimate yourself, dude," Nathaniel tells him.

Which makes me wonder, Have I been underestimating Mason?

FOURTEEN

It's Thursday morning. Part of me can't wait for forensics camp—we are going to start analyzing evidence in the case of the cafeteria vandal today—but another part of me wishes I could just stay home and hang out with Roxie.

When I wake up, she is curled on the floor by my bed, watching me. "Hey, pal," I say to her, and I swear she smiles. I do not even mind her dog breath when she licks my face. I kiss her muzzle. That expression about a dog being man's best friend? It could be true. Right now I'm finding it hard to imagine Roxie ever being a guard dog, though Larry told us she could take down a criminal—even one who is over six feet and weighs three hundred pounds.

Mom and Dad's bedroom door is closed, so I decide to take Roxie out for a quick pee. When I pass the kitchen, I notice a wrapped present at the spot where I sit. Inside is a bracelet with a copper dog-bone charm on it. I slip it on my wrist. It may not be forensic themed, but I love it.

Outside, the air feels lighter than it has for days. Except for a woodpecker I hear at the top of a tall maple, and two squirrels scurrying across a telephone wire, the neighborhood is fast asleep. When Roxie reaches the corner, she sits and waits for my signal to cross. Her one ear is up (the other seems to be permanently flopped over).

When Mason comes to pick me up for camp, I am still admiring my new bracelet. Roxie is sitting with me on the front porch. She stands up when Mason unlatches the fence.

"Everything's good," I say, and Roxie sits back down. I can feel her watching me, waiting to see if I will give her another command.

"He sure is beautiful," Mason says. "Can I pet him? Or will he eat me?"

"Roxie is a *she*. And yes, you can pet her. She only eats bad guys. You're not *bad*—just mildly annoying."

Mason laughs. He thinks I'm teasing—and I am in too good a mood to set him straight. There is a part of me that still can't believe I have a dog. Mason kneels down and strokes the dark fur between Roxie's ears. "How can she tell the good guys from the bad guys?"

"We signal her. She's trained to respond to verbal and visual cues."

Roxie lies down on the porch and shuts her eyes. I think she likes Mason. First Nathaniel. And now Roxie. Mason is getting more popular every day.

"So what are the cues?" Mason asks. "Do you clap or wink or something?"

"I'm afraid that information is top secret."

Mom comes out to bring Roxie inside. "Congratulations on the dog, Mrs. Letour," Mason tells her. "She's a beauty."

"She certainly is," Mom says, "and she makes us feel safe. Don't you, Roxie?" Roxie thumps her tail when Mom says her name.

Even if I want Roxie to be mostly my dog, I'm glad she's Mom's too. "Thanks again for the dog-bone bracelet, Mom," I say as I start down the stairs. "Love you."

"Tab?" Mom sounds surprised. Maybe I don't tell her I love her often enough.

"Yeah?"

"Love you too," she says.

"We're picking Nathaniel up," Mason says after Mom and Roxie go inside.

"We're doing *what*?"

"Picking Nathaniel up. He's on our way."

"When exactly did you arrange that?" Just when I was getting used to our morning routine, Mason has to change things up. Bad enough I have to share the sidewalk in the afternoon, and now I am going to have the share it in the morning too.

"We texted last night."

I roll my eyes. "So now you and Nathaniel *text* each other? *Sheesh*. I never would've guessed you guys would hit it off."

"It was just a couple of texts." Mason sounds apologetic. "You and Patti text each other, don't you?"

"Your lunch bag," I remind him when we reach the fence. "Did you leave it on the steps?"

"Uh, yeah, I guess I did. What would I do without you?" Mason asks.

"You'd be lost without me! You better remember that!" I call as he jogs back for the bag.

"Hey, do you think you could speed it up a little?" I say when Mason has almost caught up with me.

Mason grins. He seems to be in an unusually good mood. "I may not be fast," he says, "but I'm strong."

When we get to Nathaniel's house, a bunch of people— there must be nearly a dozen—are milling around the front door. The rosebush has begun to lose some of its pink petals.

"Who d'you think all those people are?" I ask Mason.

"Whoever they are, they don't look too happy."

Mason has a point. Everyone looks upset. Some are talking in small clumps, shaking their heads the way people do in front of a church after a funeral. A bald man with glasses—he must be Nathaniel's grandmother's fiancé— peers up and down the street, using his hand for a visor. At first I don't see Nathaniel, but then I spot him next to a woman in yoga pants and a hoodie. It is only when she turns around that I realize it's his grandmother. She's wearing a chunky silver necklace and lots of silver bangles around one wrist. Nathaniel is patting her back.

Mason shifts from one foot to the other. "I think we might be intruding," he whispers.

"Go get Nathaniel," I insist, "or we'll be late for camp."

Just as Mason is going over to Nathaniel, a police car screeches to a halt at the curb. The officer who steps out from the driver's side looks like an older version of Nathaniel, with the same dark hair and brooding eyes. "I just heard," he says in a voice that is lower than Nathaniel's but just as gruff.

I move in closer to hear what is going on. From what I can tell, Nathaniel's dad was on patrol when he got a call that there was a robbery at his own house. Automatically, I find myself looking at the house for signs of forced entry—but I do not see any. Just as I am wondering what the thief—or thieves—got away with, I hear Nathaniel's grandmother say, "I only left him outside for a minute, when I realized I forgot the poop bag."

Which is when I realize it is Nathaniel's grandmother's Pomeranian that was stolen. My chest tightens. I have only been a dog owner for a few days, but I already know how devastated I'd be if something happened to Roxie. I can hardly remember what my life was like before I got her. I need Roxie. And for the first time, it occurs to me that feeling needy is not always such a bad thing.

"How do you know he didn't just take off?" Nathaniel's dad asks.

"Don't be ridiculous, André!" It feels strange to hear a gray-haired woman in yoga pants shouting at an officer in uniform, but of course that officer must be her son. Though their hair is not the same color, they have the same dark eyes as Nathaniel. "Willy would never run away! Your father trained him never to leave the yard." So she's definitely his mother. "Willy was stolen! You told me yourself there have been several dognappings in Montreal recently." Her voice breaks on the word *dognappings*.

The bald guy pushes his way through the crowd toward Nathaniel's grandmother. When he puts his arm around her shoulders, Nathaniel backs away a few steps and wipes his cheek. I wonder if he has been crying. I would not have expected him to be the kind of kid who would get attached to a dog, especially such a small one. Then again, I never expected him to get friendly with Mason.

"Look, Mother," Nathaniel's father says, "I know you're upset. I know you love that dog. Fred," he says to the fiancé, "let's go inside so I can take a report. I don't have much time. And I have to be honest with you, Mother—missing dogs are not the police department's highest priority."

When Nathaniel's grandmother starts to sob, Fred strokes the back of her head.

I decide it is time for me and Mason to bolt—with or without Nathaniel. But when I look for Mason, I realize that he has gone to talk to Nathaniel's grandmother. He is actually offering her the juice box from his lunch bag—and she is smiling back at him. Who knew that besides Mason's remarkable ability to haul 150-pound dummies he was also good at comforting senior citizens?

"That's very kind of you." Nathaniel's grandmother sniffles. "Are you Mason? Nathaniel's friend from forensics camp?" Then she suddenly seems to remember Nathaniel is there too. "You should go to camp, dear. I know today's a big day. Didn't you say you were analyzing evidence?"

"Are you sure you're going to be all right, Grandma?" Nathaniel asks her.

"I'll be fine"—she waves one hand in the air, and the silver bracelets make a jingling sound—"once we get Willy back."

Fred ruffles Nathaniel's hair. "Try to have a good day at camp, son."

Nathaniel doesn't answer. He ducks to get out of Fred's reach. Mason catches my eye. He has also noticed Nathaniel's reaction.

Something tells me Mason and I are thinking the same thing—Fred's a decent guy. But neither of us voices the thought. Nathaniel would not want to hear it

Even when we are halfway down his block, Nathaniel looks back at his house as if he is hoping Willy will have come home.

"That sucks about your grandmother's dog," Mason says for both of us.

"I just got a dog—a German shepherd," I add, though they are not paying attention to me.

"We'll help you get Willy back," Mason says.

"We will? I mean, of course we will," I say.

"The thing about Willy"—Nathaniel pauses, and I wonder if he is trying not to cry—"is that when he's running around the yard, or jumping on the bed, well, it feels like Grandpa's still here."

I don't know what to say to that, so I am relieved when Mason comes up with something. "It sounds like you and your grandpa were pretty close."

"Very," Nathaniel says.

Because those two have basically forgotten about *moi*, I have time to think. I think of Nathaniel's dad's gruff voice and his impatience with his own mother. Nathaniel's dad is probably not a person who is easy to talk to—even if you're his kid. Maybe that's why Nathaniel misses his grandpa so much. Maybe his grandpa was a softer sort of person. Someone who listened.

I look at the T-shirt Nathaniel has on today. It is black with a giant white skull in the middle and, underneath it, a set of crossbones. For the first time it occurs to me that maybe Nathaniel's fixation on skulls and crossbones isn't because he's into blood and gore. It's about death.

FIFTEEN

Samantha and Lloyd exchange worried looks when we tell them about Nathaniel's grandmother's dog. They look even more concerned when we say there have been other dognappings in the city in the last few weeks and that the police department does not consider the missing dogs a priority.

Stacey notices their reaction too. "Do you guys have dogs?" she asks them.

"I don't," Samantha says. Then she adds, "Allergies," as if she needs to explain why someone would not have a dog.

"Me neither. Our apartment building doesn't allow them." Lloyd's forehead creases, which makes me wonder if something is troubling him. "But I grew up around dogs. My brother was a dog person." When Lloyd uses the word *was*, I shiver. His brother must be dead. Judging by Lloyd's age, the brother could not have been very old when he died. "Those missing dogs," Lloyd says. "You don't happen to know if they were purebreds, do you?"

I picture the posters I've seen. A Chihuahua, a standard poodle...and now Nathaniel's grandmother's Pomeranian. And didn't Larry say he had heard someone was stealing purebred dogs? "I think so," I tell Lloyd.

"Hmm..." is all Lloyd says. When he rubs his forehead a few times, I know for sure that something is bugging him.

At first, probably because we are all thinking about the missing dogs, it's hard to focus on the case of the vandalized cafeteria. Samantha makes four columns on the whiteboard, one for each suspect. She puts their initials at the top: L.T. for Leo Tessier, the chef; A.L. for Amelia Lester, his assistant; J.C. for Jonah Cartwright, the student; and M.L. for Ming Lu. Or Mrs. Lu. Either way, the *M* works.

Samantha adds the words *evidence* and *possible motives* to the left side of the whiteboard.

"Excuse me," I say. "How come we're looking at possible motives? Didn't you guys tell us forensic scientists don't try to figure out the why? That that's a detective's job?"

"You're right—technically," Samantha says. "We're just trying to make forensics camp as interesting as possible."

"It's working!" Mason calls out. "This camp is definitely interesting. I'm liking it as much as cooking camp." Coming from Mason, that's a big compliment.

Lloyd waves his cell phone at Samantha, signaling that he has to leave the room to make a call. "Give me ten minutes," I hear him tell Samantha in a low voice as he slips out of the conference room.

Samantha's eyes follow Lloyd as he closes the door behind him. I think she is worried about him. But when she turns back to us, she is all business again.

"This morning," Samantha says, "we're going to apply Locard's Exchange Principle to our case. Let's start by making a list of trace evidence that might have been taken from the scene, as well as trace evidence that was left. Can any of you think of evidence that could have been *taken*?"

"Willy," Nathaniel says quietly. "Willy was taken."

"Willy?" Samantha says. "What are you talking about, Nathaniel?"

Nathaniel bites his lip. "Sorry, I must have been thinking out loud."

"Willy is his grandmother's dog," I explain. I stop myself from adding, *The one who got dognapped*. Nathaniel is already upset, and I am trying not to make things worse.

Samantha sits down at the table with the rest of us. "Look," she says, resting her elbows on the table, "I'm going to level with you. I really wish there was some way we could help you find Willy. And don't forget that it is always possible he and the other dogs ran away. If that's the case, then chances are good they'll be found and returned to their owners. If—and it's a big if—there is evidence the dogs were dognapped, then we would have to leave the case to the professionals. Either way, Lloyd and I were hired to teach you guys about forensics, not help you investigate missing dogs." She sighs in a way that makes me think she might be disappointed too.

"But what if the dogs *were* dognapped and the professionals don't do anything?" Mason asks. "Nathaniel's dad is a cop, and we heard him say missing dogs aren't a priority for the police department."

Samantha shakes her head. "I don't know what to tell you—except that it's too soon to jump to conclusions. And one more thing. If you focus on what you're learning this week at forensics camp, and if some of you are serious about going into the field, well then, one day you might be able to use the skills you've acquired here to solve real cases. Like dognappings. If that's what these are. But you're not there yet. So what do you say we get back to my chart?" Samantha goes back to her spot in front of the whiteboard.

I try to focus on Samantha's chart. Across the table, Mason straightens his back and studies the chart too.

But Nathaniel is staring out the window. "Nathaniel?" Samantha says. He yawns as he turns back to face her.

"I just realized there's something Lloyd and I forgot to mention," Samantha says. "Not every group of campers is able to solve their case. Sometimes they come up empty— which is disappointing, of course—and Lloyd and I have to reveal the culprit."

Nathaniel swivels closer to the conference table. "We'll solve the case," he says.

When we turn our attention back to Samantha's chart, we agree that, as far as we know, no trace evidence was removed from the cafeteria. Mason and Nathaniel report that they found forty dollars in the cash register. It is a sign that our suspect is a vandal, not a thief.

"Unless the vandal grabbed a slice on his way out," Nico says. "Or a yogurt."

No one laughs.

It is way easier to come up with the list of trace evidence *left* at the scene. We start with the fingerprints we found on the counter and the freezer-door handle. "And we still need to dust the mustard container for prints," Muriel says.

"Unfortunately, that probably won't work. The mustard container is textured plastic, and it's hard to get prints off a bumpy plastic surface," Samantha says.

Stacey shakes her head each time Samantha says the word *plastic*.

Nico mentions the footprints that were on the kitchen floor.

"We'll need to get all of your footwear impressions so we can rule those out," Samantha explains. She has started another list, this one of stuff we need to work on today. "Nico and Stacey, I'm putting the two of you in charge of taking footwear impressions."

We are still discussing footwear—Samantha is explaining that Nico and Stacey will use tubs of sand and plaster of Paris to take everyone's impressions—when Lloyd returns to the conference room, shutting the door behind him. He and Samantha do not speak, but she catches Lloyd's eye and raises her eyebrows, as if she is asking a question. When Lloyd shrugs, I know the answer is that he is not sure.

"Why don't we have a look at your photos of the crime scene?" Lloyd asks. Mason and Nathaniel take out their cameras, and the rest of us huddle around. Stacey makes a clucking sound when she sees a photo of the coffee cup Muriel and I found in the garbage. "The exterior is paper, but the inside is plastic-coated," Stacey says. And we know how she feels about plastic.

Samantha adds *coffee cup* to the list of trace evidence left at the scene.

"Not that I approve of plastic-coated cups," I say, looking at Stacey before I turn back to Samantha, "but is it any easier to get prints off a smooth coffee cup than a bumpy mustard container?"

"As a matter of fact, it is," Samantha says. "After we've had our snack break, you and Muriel might try dusting that cup. All right then, do you guys have anything else to add to our list?"

Mason nudges Nathaniel. At first I think it has something to do with the coffee cup, but then Nathaniel fishes a small brown paper bag out of his front pocket. The bag is folded over and sealed. "We found this at the crime scene," Nathaniel says.

Lloyd raises his eyebrows. "So why didn't you show it to us then?"

Nathaniel gives Lloyd the bag. "We, uh…we thought it would be cool to present a piece of surprise evidence. Like they do on TV."

Lloyd examines the bag. Mason and Nathaniel have recorded the date, time and location of their find. "Nice forensics work on the labeling," he tells Mason and Nathaniel. "But from now on, you need to remember that you're all one team.

This isn't about being some kind of TV star; this is forensics. You guys"—now Lloyd looks at the six of us—"are going to need to work together to solve this puzzle."

Lloyd cuts open the paper bag, has a look inside, then passes the bag around so we can all see it. Inside is a single hair. The hair is black, straight as a stick and four inches long (the measurement is also included on the label).

I nearly raise my hand again. "I think this hair belongs to Mrs. Lu. Her hair is straight, black and medium-length. And she admitted she doesn't like working at the cafeteria. I think Mrs. Lu is the vandal."

Stacey is not convinced. "Mrs. Lu's hair has gray streaks."

"Only in the front," I say. "This hair could have come from the back of her head."

Samantha adds *strand of hair* to our list of trace evidence, and then, in the space for possible motives, she writes that Mrs. Lu dislikes her job at the cafeteria.

"They all dislike their jobs," Nathaniel says.

"Not Jonah Cartwright," Nico corrects him. "Jonah doesn't *have* a job."

"Yeah, but Jonah has a prior history," Muriel calls out. "He's been in trouble for vandalism before."

Samantha writes *prior history/vandalism* in the box for Jonah Cartwright's possible motive. Then she adds *dislikes job* under *possible motives* for both Amelia Lester and Leo Tessier.

"I don't think Leo Tessier did it," Stacey says.

"Why not?" Nico asks her. "There's something suspicious about his mustache. Do you think he glues it on?"

Stacey does not realize Nico is joking. "The mustache is definitely real. I just don't think a man who likes meat as much as he does would leave it to rot on the cafeteria floor."

"Good point," Muriel says.

Nico raises one finger in the air. "Maybe the meat was past its best-before date."

"That's another good point," Samantha says. "Didn't you and Stacey check the labels?"

"All we got was the weight," Nico tells her. "The ink on the labels was too runny to read the rest."

There is still a little time before snack break, so Samantha and Lloyd show us images of the fingerprints we lifted from the counter and the freezer. There are four different fingerprints. We are getting faster at identifying whorls, loops and arches.

"Nice work," Samantha tells us. "Now we have something else to show you—fingerprints for each of the four suspects."

"When did you get those?" Muriel asks.

"Last week," Lloyd answers. "You guys were on summer holiday, but Samantha and I were busy preparing for forensics camp."

"Can we see Mrs. Lu's first?" I ask. I still think she might be our culprit.

Samantha puts Mrs. Lu's fingerprints up on the screen. I see that some of them are arched, like mine. When Samantha puts them next to the fingerprints we found at the scene, I realize I am breathing hard. All four fingerprints seem to be Mrs. Lu's! We've got a match!

"I told you so!" I say to the others. "The hair, her complaints about her job, and now these prints. I bet you anything Mrs. Lu did it! Maybe she even washed the grease trap on purpose—to get rid of the evidence."

"Whoa, Tabitha!" Samantha says. "Not so fast!" I remember Lloyd saying I'm a fast walker. I guess I'm a fast thinker too. "It is possible that Mrs. Lu vandalized the cafeteria, but don't forget that she also could have left her prints when she was cleaning the cafeteria."

"If she was cleaning, wouldn't she have worn gloves or wiped off her fingerprints?" Nathaniel asks, and I have to admit I wish I had come up with that question.

Samantha thinks about that for a moment. "What I'm saying is, it's too soon in our investigation to say with any certainty that Mrs. Lu did it." Samantha pauses. I know she is about to say something important, maybe share a fact we have been overlooking. Instead she adds, "Besides, it's only Thursday morning."

SIXTEEN

We eat our snacks at a picnic table outside the Life Sciences Building. Samantha and Lloyd are deep in conversation at another table, probably planning our next activity.

Nathaniel does not bother opening his bag of trail mix. When he catches Mason eyeing it, Nathaniel slides it over to him. "All yours, dude," he says. Nathaniel checks his cell phone for messages. When he sighs, I know it means there is no news about Willy.

Nico plays pretend piano on the picnic table, his fingers tapping on invisible keys.

I nudge Muriel. "Does he play piano for real?" I ask her. I would not have pegged Nico as the musical type.

Muriel snorts. "Playing piano requires the ability to concentrate. Nico only plays tables."

Nico sweeps the back of his hands against the picnic table to indicate his imaginary performance is over. Then he looks up at us. "I still say the chef did it," he says. "So he could get a day off and apply for a job at a decent restaurant," he says.

"It's not much of a motive," I say. "Couldn't he just have taken a sick day?"

"Maybe he used them all up," Nico says. "Or how about this? Maybe he wanted publicity for the cafeteria. He seems like the kind of person who needs a lot of attention."

"You would know," Muriel says.

Nico, Muriel and Stacey each have two pieces of string cheese and a box of raisins. Stacey finishes her cheese before she starts on the raisins. She must like keeping food separate in her stomach too.

Nico tears a strip off the cheese and holds it over his lip so it looks like a pale yellow mustache. "Now who do I remind you of?" he asks.

"Why are you such a dork?" Muriel asks him.

"It's in my genes. Which happen to be your genes too."

"And mine." Stacey shakes her head, but I can tell from the way she is pursing her lips that she's trying not to laugh. "I think we can rule the chef out. Not just because of the meat, but also because his fingerprints haven't turned up anywhere."

"We haven't dusted the coffee cup." I make a point of not using the words *plastic-coated* or *nonrecyclable*. That would only set Stacey off again. "Or examined the footwear evidence."

Suddenly Nathaniel bangs his fist on the picnic table so hard he sends my water bottle flying. "Sorry about that," he says, reaching over to pick up the bottle, which is now half empty. "But can we please stop talking about some made-up case? Especially when there's a real case right in front us, begging to be solved."

The picnic table is still vibrating when Stacey says, "Samantha told us to leave the real case to the police." Her voice is calm and firm. It's the tone people use when they are convinced they are right. Mrs. Johnson uses that tone a lot. "Besides," Stacey adds, "we don't want to be the kind of campers who can't solve their own case."

Nathaniel straightens his shoulders. "We'll solve the cafeteria case," he says. "But we all know the police aren't going to do anything about the missing dogs."

I am thinking about Willy and the other missing dogs. Who knows how many there are? Some people must just assume their dogs have run away. Where are they, and are they safe and being well treated? What if some are on special diets, the way Roxie is? How would the dognapper know what to feed them? "Maybe we could at least do a little investigating…" I say. "Nothing dangerous," I add quickly.

"I don't think it's a good idea," Stacey says. "We're just a bunch of kids."

"A bunch of smart kids," Nico says. "Okay, I'll admit it, maybe I'm not that smart. But you guys are."

Stacey looks over to the table where Samantha and Lloyd are sitting. "They wouldn't be happy about it."

Nathaniel leans across the table toward Stacey and drops his voice. "They don't need to know. But like Lloyd told us, it takes a team to solve a case. Unless we're all in, this isn't gonna work." He looks Stacey in the eye. "So what do you say?"

"I don't know," Stacey answers.

"We'd just be doing reconnaissance," I tell her. I have always liked the sound of the word *reconnaissance*, but this is the first time I have ever been able to use it in real life. "If we learn anything, we'll pass the information on to Nathaniel's father. Right, Nathaniel?"

Now Nathaniel looks at me. When he does, I'm pretty sure he has no intention of passing any information on to his father. "Right," he says. "Let's review what we know so far."

Stacey whips out her forensic-science notebook so she can start a fresh list.

"What we know so far is that a Chihuahua, a standard poodle and a Pomeranian are missing. All purebreds," Nathaniel says.

Stacey writes the word *purebreds*, underlining it so hard I am sure she is leaving an imprint on the next page.

I tell the others about Larry and how he warned us to keep an eye on Roxie because he had heard there was a dognapper on the loose.

Nathaniel is perking up. "Let me get this straight. You've got a German shepherd—a purebred?"

"Yup. Roxie. She's a beauty. Ask Mason—the two of them hit it off."

Nathaniel is not interested in hearing Mason's opinion of Roxie. "We might be able to use Roxie as bait," he says.

"No way," I tell him. "Don't even think about it!"

Stacey raises one finger in the air. "I thought we weren't going to do anything dangerous."

"We're not," Nathaniel tells her.

"What we need to do is apply Locard's Exchange Principle," Mason says, "and even if we aren't detectives, we should consider possible motives."

"He's right." There I go, agreeing with Mason again! What is going on here?

"I can only think of a couple of reasons why anyone would steal dogs. One would be"—Mason glances at Nathaniel—"for animal experiments. Sorry, Nathaniel. The other reason—and the one that's more likely—is for profit. Maybe the dognapper is reselling purebreds for less than breeders do. I bet lots of people would be interested and not ask too many questions."

Great deals on purebred dogs? Why didn't I think of it before? The Kijiji ad my dad and I saw when we were looking for a guard dog! I am so eager to tell the others that I start blabbering. "This ad! On Kijiji! My dad and I…we saw this ad! On Kijiji!"

"Could you calm down a little?" Muriel says.

Muriel's cell phone is in front of her on the picnic table. "Do you get the Internet on that thing?" I ask.

"Of course I do," she says. "I've got three gigabytes of data," she adds proudly.

She is about to explain how data is measured when somehow I manage to say, "Google Kijiji + Montreal + pure-bred dogs. Now!"

The first listing is the one my dad and I saw. Muriel reads the information out loud: "*Amazing deals on purebred dogs of all kinds, Montreal.*"

Nico whistles. "We need to get in touch with this guy right away and set up a meeting."

Stacey is gripping the edge of the picnic table like it is a ledge she is about to fall off of. "Going online to set up a meeting doesn't sound very safe to me."

"Don't worry," Nico says. "It'll be safe—Muriel will take care of it."

SEVENTEEN

I need to refill my water bottle. There is a water fountain in front of the Life Sciences Building. Lloyd and Samantha are so busy talking they don't even notice when I walk by. Aren't forensic scientists supposed to be observant at all times?

"He doesn't have a cell phone?" Samantha is saying to Lloyd. "I thought everyone had a cell phone. I saw a photo online of a Masai warrior in Kenya—even he had a cell phone."

"Well, he doesn't—and I'm pretty sure he's back on the street. He comes home once in a while. He goes back to working at the vet's and everything seems to be okay, but then he takes off again. It's as if the streets have a hold on him, but I don't think it's drugs."

Samantha sighs. "I'm sorry, Lloyd. It must be really hard for you and your parents."

"It is. But it's harder for Sebastian."

So Lloyd's brother is not dead. He lives on the streets. In a city as big as Montreal, I am used to seeing street people. I just never knew any personally or knew anyone else who did.

Lloyd looks down at the grass. When he looks up, he notices me. I hope he doesn't realize I have overheard such a private conversation. "Everything okay? It looked like Nathaniel was getting a little worked up before."

"We were just arguing about whether Mrs. Lu did it," I say quickly.

Samantha pats Lloyd's elbow. "I guess that means forensics camp is going well," she tells him.

Lloyd raises his juice box into the air. "Here's to *everything* going well." I wonder if he is thinking about his brother.

When I get back from the water fountain, Muriel has already opened a new Gmail account and messaged the guy from Kijiji to say she is interested in buying a pure-bred Chihuahua. At first she was going to say she wanted a Pomeranian, but Nathaniel ruled that out. Nathaniel's thinking was that if this guy was the dognapper, he might get suspicious if the dog Muriel wanted happened to be the last kind of dog that went missing. The dognapper might figure we were trying to set him up.

"Are you sure it's safe?" Stacey is asking.

"That's why Muriel created a new Gmail account." Nico is playing pretend piano again. "Did the guy message you back yet?" he asks his sister.

Muriel checks her cell phone. "No new emails. All we can do now is sit tight." She eyes Nico's fingers. "I know that's hard for you."

Nathaniel stretches his arms when he stands up. "C'mon, you guys," he says. "Let's go figure out who vandalized the cafeteria. Unless you want to let Lloyd and Samantha solve the case for us."

Because we have a lot of evidence to analyze, Lloyd and Samantha take us to the forensics laboratory. The lab is locked, probably because there is so much expensive equipment inside: microscopes, a gas chromatograph (a device that breaks down and identifies chemicals), and a machine that replicates DNA until you have a large enough amount to study.

There are three gleaming stainless-steel sinks for us to work at and a long counter where Nico and Stacey will be able to work on footwear impressions.

In a corner, a tall skeleton dangles from the ceiling. When the sunlight lands on it, the skeleton shimmers. If we were anywhere else, the skeleton would be a leftover Halloween decoration. But not here. Here, that thing could be real. The thought makes me get a little shivery. Why am I not surprised when Nathaniel walks right over to the skeleton and stands in front of it like he is mesmerized?

Mason helps Samantha lug a bag of plaster of Paris over to the counter. When that is done, he walks over to Nathaniel. "You okay, dude?" he asks. Mason never used to say *dude*. He must have picked it up from Nathaniel.

"D'you ever wonder what happens to people after they… you know—die?" Nathaniel asks Mason.

Mason pauses the way he does when he is looking for the right words. "I don't know for sure, but if you ask me, there's got to be more to us than this." He runs his fingertip along one of the skeleton's thin ribs.

"Sometimes it feels like my grandfather's in the room," Nathaniel says. "Not now. But other times. Not like a ghost or anything. Just…well…kind of present."

Nico and Stacey are at one of the sinks, helping Samantha mix plaster powder with water. "We're coming to get your footwear impressions!" Stacey's voice echoes in the lab.

Muriel and I are at a workstation, dusting the coffee cup for prints. The surface is rounded, but Muriel is getting good at using the wand. She is not wasting much of the metallic powder. Between the sunlight streaming in through the windows and the overhead fluorescents, the lab is bright, making it easier for us to see two fingerprints emerge from the magnetic powder.

"We see something!" I call out, and when I wave everyone over, I bump into Muriel. The cup flies out of her hand, but luckily she catches it with her other hand. I hold my breath while she checks that the fingerprints are not spoiled.

Nico brings two tubs of sand over to us. "It's me, Prince Charming," he says. "Does one of you happen to be Cinderella? Because I'd like to see your shoes."

I laugh, mostly because I'm relieved we didn't lose those fingerprints.

"So did you ever read the version of the story where Prince Charming was a forensic scientist?" Nico asks.

Muriel and I each step into—and out of—the tubs of sand. Nico pours the plaster of Paris mixture over my footwear impression in the sand. The plaster casts need time to dry before we can see if the impressions came out clearly. Stacey and Nico have already got Nathaniel's and Mason's impressions. They still need Samantha's and Lloyd's—and also their own.

Mrs. Lu knocks at the lab door. "You wanted to see us?" she says to the counselors.

Leo Tessier is behind her. So is Amelia Lester, and now I see that Jonah Cartwright is there too. It feels weird to see all our suspects together, in person, like they have stepped out of the video the counselors showed us—which in a way they have.

"Thanks for coming," Lloyd tells them. "As you know, we've already got your fingerprints on file. But now our footwear team would like to take your footwear impressions. And we'll also need a handwriting sample." Lloyd looks over at us. "Is there anything else you'd like to ask our visitors?"

Muriel's hand flies up into the air, but then, just as quickly, she drops it down again.

"Muriel?" Lloyd says.

"Umm," Muriel says, "would it be rude if we asked the visitors to leave for a minute?"

"Bah!" Mrs. Lu says. "I see more rude behavior than that in the cafeteria all the time." She pulls Leo by the string on the back of his apron.

Amelia follows Leo. "I don't understand why you're so opposed to mushroom stew," we hear her tell him.

Leo throws his hands up in the air. "Everyone knows that stew requires beef!" he mutters, without bothering to turn around and face Amelia.

Stacey nudges me. "See what I mean?" she whispers.

Jonah is the last of our suspects to leave the laboratory. "Those two aren't much fun to be around," he says, pointing with his chin at Leo and Amelia. "Let us know when you're ready for us to come back," he adds before he shuts the door behind him.

Lloyd sits down on a tall stool. "All right, Muriel. Tell us what you're thinking."

There is a spot of black powder on the tip of Muriel's nose. "I think we should ask them each to do a short spelling test. And we should include the word *meat*—the kind you buy from a butcher."

Now why didn't I think of that?

It is proof that it takes a team to solve a crime.

EIGHTEEN

When we call the cafeteria staff back in, Leo and Amelia tell us they are in a hurry. Apparently, they need to discuss next week's menus. I have a feeling the discussion is going to end in an argument. Muriel and I agree to take a break from our fingerprinting assignment to help get their footwear impressions.

"Meat farms are destroying this planet," Amelia tells Leo.

"Nonsense." Leo still won't look at her.

Those two don't make much of a team—and I don't think they're acting. I think their problem is they both want to be right. Or maybe they're just not team players.

As for me, I may not be used to being a team player—probably because I'm an only child—but I'm starting to like it. Working together toward a common goal is fun. I wonder if honeybees feel the same way when they collect pollen and nectar.

Mrs. Lu is peering through one of the microscopes at a piece of human bone. "What are those little boxes?" she asks Samantha.

"You mean the rectangles, right? Those are osteons," Samantha explains. I can tell right away that she loves talking about human remains. "They are made up of osteocytes. Osteons are present in many bones of most mammals."

"Osteons. Osteons." Mrs. Lu says it twice. She must like the sound of the word.

"Mrs. Lu," Stacey says, "if you don't mind stepping into this vat. It will only take a minute."

Muriel is getting Leo's footwear impressions. He is wearing bright-orange runners, which I had not noticed under his baggy white chef's pants. He is asking Muriel about forensics camp—and I notice he is being a lot friendlier to her than to Amelia. "It makes me wish I was a keed again," he tells Muriel. "You say each one of our fingers has a different fingerprint? I assumed zay were all the same."

Amelia is less talkative than her boss. When he is not looking, she rolls her eyes at him. "*It makes me wish I was a keed again*," she whispers, imitating his accent. "If that man is so interested in keeds, he should offer healthier meal choices for the university students. In a few years from now, some of them will be having their own keeds."

"He didn't say he was interested in kids," I point out. "He said he wished he could be a kid again."

Amelia is wearing a pair of blue-and-white leather shoes that look like they came from a vintage store too. After I get her footwear impressions, she kicks the side of the plastic vat to make sure all the sand is off. I check the impression I just took and say, "I think you might have a piece of gum or a pebble or something at the top of your right shoe."

Amelia takes the shoe off and totters on the other leg. "You're right about the gum. That's kinda cool."

Lloyd has gone to get paper and pens. "Before you go," he tells the suspects, "Muriel would like to take handwriting samples." He does not say anything about a spelling test, which I decide is probably a wise move. I am guessing that because English is not Leo's or Mrs. Lu's first language, they might have trouble spelling—and they might be embarrassed if they knew this was a spelling test. If I'm right, and one of them spells the meat you buy at a butcher shop with two *e*'s, then our case could be solved!

Muriel gives each suspect paper and a pen. They are sitting on metal stools at the long counter. I have pushed the vats with the footwear impressions over to the side. Muriel makes sure there is enough space between each suspect that they will not be able to look at each other's answers.

"All right…" Muriel turns to me, and I know she is scrambling for what to do next. "If you could number your sheets one to ten, please. And if you could please write in cursive."

"Cursive?" Mrs. Lu asks..

"Yes, you know—like this. With the letters linked." Muriel scribbles her name on a sheet and holds it up to show Mrs. Lu. "The first word is…" Muriel hesitates.

"Bake," I call out.

Leo Tessier twirls his mustache. "It's one of my favorite words," he says.

"Please write it with a capital *B*," I add. It will be useful to see how the suspects write their capital *B*s, since that is how the mustard message starts out.

"Right," Muriel says. "In fact, that's your second word. *Right*. As opposed to left. Or wrong."

We give them the words *hotter* (that will show us how they cross their *t*'s), *dogs* (because I am thinking about Roxie and wondering what she is up to while I am at forensics camp), *recycle* (in case Stacey is listening), *skull* (that one is for Nathaniel), *Bob* (which will give us another capital *B* to look at), *lessons* (we almost forgot that we also need to see some *s*'s) and *Montreal* (because it's the best city in the world and it has a capital *M*).

The last word is *Meat*. Muriel explains she means the kind of meat you buy at a butcher shop.

Jonah crinkles his nose as he writes the word. Amelia sighs. Leo smiles. He must be thinking of *rôti de boeuf*. Mrs. Lu throws her pencil down on the counter when she is done.

I should get back to the fingerprinting station, but I cannot resist looking over the suspects' shoulders to see how they have spelled *Meat*.

I am closest to Jonah. He has spelled the word correctly. Same for Amelia. I lean in to get a better view of Leo's paper. He has spelled the word correctly too. Which leaves Mrs. Lu.

Something tells me we are coming close to solving this case.

But when I look at Mrs. Lu's sheet, I see that she, too, has spelled the word correctly.

How can that be?

Our four suspects file out of the room. Amelia and Leo seem to have stopped speaking to each other altogether. "See ya later," I hear Jonah tell Samantha. They must be friends. Mrs. Lu picks up a piece of dried plaster from the floor and drops it in the garbage can on her way out. She and my dad would definitely get along.

I take another look at Mrs. Lu's sheet. Maybe I saw wrong.

Then I remember Samantha warning us about not trying to jam the puzzle pieces together. Is that what I have been trying to do?

We also have index cards with each suspect's ten fingerprints. Muriel and I need to identify those two thumbprints on the paper cup. We start with Mrs. Lu's card, but we do not get a match. "I really thought it would be her," I tell Muriel.

It looks as if one of the thumbprints belongs to Leo. And that the other one belongs to Amelia.

"Why would both of their thumbprints be on the same cup?" Muriel wonders out loud.

"She could have passed his coffee to him. Or the other way around," I say.

Muriel slaps the top of her head. "Why didn't I think of that?"

"Because you're the computer whiz. Which leaves me in charge of paper cups." I take a bow, and Muriel laughs.

Stacey and Nico are at the other end of the room. "Any results yet on the footwear evidence?" I call out to them. The counselors have printed up enlarged photographs of the footprints found on the kitchen floor, and Stacey and Lloyd are comparing those with the photos taken of the plaster of Paris casts.

"Not yet," Stacey answers. "It's possible that our suspect changed his—or her—shoes after committing the crime."

"What about the handwriting?" Muriel asks Mason and Nathaniel.

The two of them are hunched over the suspects' tests, comparing them to the photograph of the mustard message. "Notice how round Jonah's *B* is," Nathaniel is saying. "The *B* in the mustard message is way more angular."

"Maybe that's what happens when you use a mustard container for a pen," Mason points out.

Samantha and Lloyd are circulating quietly in the lab while we analyze evidence. "You guys are making excellent progress," Samantha tells us. "Thanks to Muriel and Tabitha's findings, we seem to be narrowing our field of suspects. Now you are going to have to continue working as a team if you want to identify our vand—"

A low buzzing noise interrupts her. The sound is coming from Muriel's backpack, where she keeps her cell phone.

Maybe the dognapper is phoning.

The five of us all turn to Muriel. Stacey's hand is over her heart.

Except for the buzzing cell phone, the room has gone totally quiet.

"Don't you want to check who's calling?" Lloyd asks Muriel.

"Nah," Muriel says nonchalantly. "It's probably a telemarketer."

Stacey drops her hand back to her side.

The buzzing has stopped, but a moment later it starts up again. Whoever it is really wants Muriel to pick up her phone.

Samantha raises her eyebrows. She must have noticed all of us turning to look at Muriel. "Is something going on here that Lloyd and I don't know about?"

"Of course not," Muriel says.

"No way," I add.

"Hey, aren't third-year forensics students supposed to know everything?" Nico asks. For once, his corny humor comes in handy. Samantha and Lloyd look at each other and chuckle. The buzzing finally stops, and the uncomfortable moment is over.

NINETEEN

I almost forget to eat my lunch because Muriel is setting up a meeting with a guy who might be our dognapper.

He wants to meet her at eight tonight at a small park on Lansdowne Avenue in Westmount.

Stacey shakes her head. "At night in some deserted park? I don't like the sound of it."

"Is he bringing the Chihuahua?" Nathaniel asks.

Muriel rolls her eyes. "Of course he's bringing the Chihuahua. The reason I'm meeting him is so I can decide about the Chihuahua."

Muriel's phone jiggles on the picnic table when it vibrates to indicate there is a new email. "Is it him?" we all ask at the same time.

Muriel reads us the new message. "*If you decide you would like to take the dog, I will require payment in cash. It's two hundred dollars, and the price is not negotiable. Hope that's okay. Please confirm that you will be at the park at eight tonight.*"

"Where am I supposed to get two hundred dollars from?" Muriel asks.

"You're not going to need the money," Nathaniel tells her. "We'll catch the guy before he can ask for the cash."

Stacey pushes her baby carrots away from her snow peas. "Catch the guy? Are you nuts?" she says to Nathaniel. "What if he's armed?"

"Relax," Nathaniel tells her. "This guy won't be armed. He's a dognapper, not a serial killer."

"I agree with Nathaniel," Muriel says. "A serial killer would not say, *Hope that's okay*. This guy's polite."

Stacey rolls her eyes. "When was the last time you hung out with a serial killer, Muriel?"

"Okay, you two, calm down," Nathaniel says, coming to stand between the two cousins. "Stacey, you seem to be forgetting that we have a secret weapon."

"A secret weapon?" I ask.

"Yeah, your dog. Roxie, right? Well, Roxie's coming."

"I told you, I don't know if that's—"

Nathaniel does not let me finish my sentence. "I thought we were a team," he says, looking me in the eye.

None of us can argue with that. Not me, and not even Stacey. We might all be very different, but Nathaniel's right—we are a team.

Stacey lives around the corner from Lansdowne Avenue. She and the twins will tell Stacey's parents they are going to meet up for ice cream with friends from forensics camp. "I'm going to leave a note on my pillow saying where we've gone," Stacey says. "In case something goes wrong."

Nathaniel waves his hand in the air. "Nothing's going to go wrong."

Mason will come to my house at seven twenty. He's going to suggest we take Roxie for a walk, and then we'll head for the park too. We should make it there by ten to eight.

"My parents might get suspicious if they see me hanging out with you of my own free will," I say, but Mason is too busy peeling the lid off his applesauce to be insulted.

Muriel uses Google Street View to show us what the park looks like up close, and Mason makes a sketch of it in his notebook.

"All six of us can't show up at the same time," Mason points out, "because if this guy really is up to no good, he might take off. I'd say there should only be a couple of us at the park. The rest need to hide out in the vicinity. Let's zoom in to scope out possible hiding spots."

Nathaniel says no one at his house will even notice if he slips out. I wonder what that would be like. "It'd be different if my grandpa was around," he mutters.

We only get half an hour in the forensics lab after lunch before we have to be at the pool for afternoon swim. The footwear impressions are beginning to dry. Some spots have turned a dull gray.

We all put on our rubber gloves. Muriel and I take another look at the coffee cup.

"Can I see it?" Stacey asks. I expect another lecture about the evils of plastic, but instead she turns the cup slowly in her hand. "It's marked 3S," she says, showing us a notation someone has made in blue pen on the side of the cup.

"Maybe it's the coffee drinker's bra size," Nico calls out.

"Three *S*? That's not even slightly funny," Muriel tells him. "Plus it shows how little you know about girls."

"It stands for three sugars," Nathaniel says. "That's how my grandpa took his coffee."

Stacey sniffs at the cup.

"What are you smelling now?" I ask her.

Her nostrils twitch like a horse's. "Mustard," she says.

"Well, that's not a surprise," Mason says. "Muriel and Tabitha found the cup next to the mustard container."

Stacey's nostrils twitch again. "What's surprising is that the mustard smell is coming from *inside* the cup."

"Let me see it," Mason says. He is the one who spots the tiny yellow fleck on the inside of the cup. "Mustard!"

"Not so fast," Lloyd tells us. "You'll need to confirm that substance is really mustard. You can try breaking down the cup to look at the yellow substance and compare it with a known mustard sample."

"But wouldn't breaking down the cup be tampering with the evidence?" Mason asks.

We all look at Lloyd. "You have several good photo-graphs of the coffee cup," he says. "You've dusted it for prints. In some cases, evidence needs to be broken down for further examination. I'd say this qualifies as one of those cases. You with me, Samantha?"

Samantha gives Lloyd a thumbs-up. "I'm with you," she tells him.

We use scissors to cut the cup into pieces. I can feel my heart pumping as we examine the yellow fleck under the microscope. We are getting close to solving our case. "Definitely yellow," Muriel says as she looks through the microscope.

Nico pushes her away so he can take a look. "It's more like yellow-brown than yellow," he says.

"Maybe it's from that crusty bit at the end of the squeeze top," Mason suggests. "Or maybe it's just because it's dried up."

"Maybe it is." I need to stop agreeing with Mason.

Lloyd sends Mason to the small kitchen at the back of the forensics department. "I'm pretty sure I saw a squeeze bottle of yellow mustard in the fridge," Lloyd tells him.

When Mason comes back with the mustard, he squeezes a little out and puts it on a glass slide.

"What do you think?" Lloyd asks when Mason compares the two samples.

Mason does not answer right away. But when he finally says, "I think we've got a match!" the rest of us clap.

That means we now have a direct link between the mustard container and the coffee cup. Whoever wrote the mustard message must have also touched the coffee cup. But where did the coffee cup come from?

The cafeteria isn't open, but there is a coffee shop on the ground level of the sports complex, and we all decide to go down there together. The coffee shop must be on summer hours too, because it wasn't open the other day. When we get there, people are lining up for their coffee. I spot the orange running shoes first. Leo Tessier is buying coffee, and Amelia Lester is with him. She has a sour expression on her face, which makes me wonder whether they have been arguing again.

I point them out to the others.

"The cafeteria coffee must suck," Nico says. "Why else would those two buy their coffee someplace else?"

"They really shouldn't be using cups with plastic coating," Stacey mutters. "I'm going to talk to the manager and suggest they offer a discount to people who bring reusable mugs. They'd end up saving money, and it would help the planet."

Muriel and I must be thinking the same thing. "C'mon. Quick," she says, grabbing my elbow. "Let's go see how sweet they like their coffee."

But just as Muriel and I are rushing over to the counter, the fire alarm sounds. It's as if the whole sports complex is clanging—the windows, the walls, even the floors. Nico blocks his ears.

"We need to get out of here now!" Lloyd's voice echoes through the lobby of the sports complex.

"I don't smell smoke," I hear Stacey saying. "I'm sure it's just a fire drill."

"Either way, we're outta here now!" Samantha is gesturing for us to follow her.

Muriel and I look at each other. Is there time to get to the counter?

"Out of zee way!" It's Leo, with Amelia close behind him. They are leaving the building without their coffee.

TWENTY

Stacey was right about the fire alarm. It's just a drill. Even so, the university staff is taking it seriously. A woman outside the sports complex is timing how long it takes for everyone to get out. The guy from building services—the one we met at the cafeteria the other day—is directing us away from the building and onto the lawn. "Leave room for the fire truck," he bellows, even though we all know no fire truck is coming.

We all head for our usual picnic table. I wonder why people are so quick to form habits. Maybe it's because the world around us is always changing, and habits are a way to hang on to things we're familiar with. Maybe even grown-ups have trouble with change. Maybe that's why Mom is so fixated on security, and Dad can't handle mess.

Today is the second-to-last day of forensics camp, and when it is over, I am going to miss it and the friends I have made here. Nico and Muriel will fly home to Vancouver on Saturday. But they will be back next summer, and I hope I will still see Stacey and Nathaniel around. I bet Patti will like them. Even Mason is not as bad as I thought. Maybe I just resented being forced to hang out with him all these years, and I couldn't see that he has some good qualities—though I'd rather not admit that to him. Besides, I've spent so many years giving Mason a hard time, I can't really imagine treating him any differently. Another example of a habit.

Lloyd and Samantha debate what to do with us for the next half hour. Lloyd thinks there is no point going to the pool, since by the time they let us back into the building and we get changed, there will be hardly any time left for swimming. Why am I not surprised when Samantha suggests we do jumping jacks? I think she likes keeping us busy.

Mason groans when he hears about the jumping jacks. "It's much too hot for vigorous exercise," he says. "Jumping jacks could cause heat stroke."

In the end, Lloyd wins and we get half an hour of free time. Muriel checks her cell phone to see if there are any new emails from the dog guy, but there aren't. Stacey goes to talk to the manager of the coffee shop, who is having a cigarette under a birch tree.

Mason and Nathaniel are sitting across from each other at the picnic table. "What made him so special?" I hear Mason ask.

At first I think they are talking about the Pomeranian, but then I hear Nathaniel say, "I guess it's that he really *got* me. Like nobody else."

Mason does not say anything—he just nods and takes in what Nathaniel has said. Which is when I have another realization: Mason may not be a scintillating conversationalist, but he knows how to listen.

"It's different with my dad," Nathaniel says. "Sometimes I get the feeling he's *evaluating* me. Wondering if I'm tough enough to be a cop like him. Grandpa never made me feel like that. Not even once."

"Do you really want to be a cop?" Mason asks.

"I dunno. I think so. I thought so." Nathaniel kicks at the grass underneath the picnic table. "My grandpa was a science teacher. He would've thought forensics camp was cool."

When a cop car turns up outside the Life Sciences Building, I figure it has something to do with the fire drill. So I'm surprised when Nathaniel's dad comes striding out. When he stops to survey the scene, I notice he has perfect posture. Maybe they teach that at police academy. His eyes land on Nathaniel and Mason, and he curls his index finger to signal that he wants to talk to Nathaniel.

"Crap," Nathaniel mutters. "What's my dad doing here?"

I am wondering that too, only I am too far away to hear their conversation. I have to settle for observing from a distance. Nathaniel's dad appears to be asking Nathaniel something, and Nathaniel is shaking his head. Now his dad is wagging his finger. I can tell he is upset.

Samantha goes over to them and shakes Nathaniel's dad's hand. It looks like she is asking if there is something she can do to help. She does not seem intimidated about talking to a cop. Maybe forensics students take courses about dealing with the police.

Nathaniel's dad puts his hands on his hips. Now it looks like he is upset with Samantha too. And then he is raising his voice, and I can make out a few words. *Willy. Wedding. Grandpa.*

Nathaniel keeps shaking his head. When he tries to speak, his dad jabs his finger in Nathaniel's face. I don't think I would like having a cop for a father. Or this particular cop anyway.

Nathaniel's dad points at the police cruiser. Samantha says something, but Nathaniel's dad ignores her.

When Nathaniel comes back to the picnic table, we are all hoping that whatever the problem is, it's fixed. But Nathaniel hangs his head in a way I have never seen him do before. Like he is defeated. This is not the Nathaniel I am used to.

"Everything okay?" Mason asks.

"No." Nathaniel grabs his backpack from under the bench. He does not look at us when he speaks. "My dad thinks I had something to do with Willy's disappearance. He's taking me home. He says he won't let me leave until I tell him where Willy is."

"On the double now!" Nathaniel's dad calls out. "You know how I feel about waiting!"

Nathaniel runs back to his dad. His shoulders are slumped.

"That's the dumbest thing I ever heard," I say. "Why would someone dognap their own dog?"

"Technically, at least, it's not his dog. It was his grandfather's dog," Muriel says when Nathaniel is out of earshot.

"You don't really think he did it, do you?" I ask Muriel.

"He might've."

"Anything is possible," Nico adds.

"But why?" I ask.

Stacey picks up a plastic wrapper from underneath the picnic table. "He told us he's upset with his grandmother for falling in love with that guy from the bereavement group. This could be his way of getting back at her."

"I honestly don't know what to think," Mason says.

I turn to look at Mason. "I thought you two were buds."

Samantha and Lloyd come to sit down at the picnic table. "It's too bad Nathaniel had to leave," Samantha says.

"You don't honestly think he's a dognapper, do you?" I ask Samantha.

Samantha tucks some red hair behind her ear. Nathaniel's dad was rude to her, and I wonder if for once she is going to show some emotion.

"I haven't seen any evidence. But I will say Nathaniel's dad seems pretty certain Nathaniel did something with his grandmother's dog."

TWENTY-ONE

Dad is surprised when I tell him Mason has dropped by so we can take Roxie out for a walk after dinner. "I was under the impression you don't really enjoy spending time with Mason," he says when I come back inside for my hoodie. Though it got hot again during the day, the air tonight has turned chilly. It reminds me that summer will not last forever.

"I don't. I mean…I didn't. He's not as bad as I thought." As the words come out of my mouth, I realize something. I mean them.

Mom looks up from the book she is reading. "That's lovely news," she says. "I had a hunch it might happen one day. Don't forget to reactivate the alarm on your way out."

Nathaniel has not been answering his cell or responding to emails. Mason thinks Nathaniel's dad has probably confiscated his phone.

So we make a point of passing Nathaniel's house. There are pink rose petals all over the front stairs. The living-room curtains stir, and we see Nathaniel's grandmother peering out the window as if she is expecting to see Willy. She waves when we pass. There is no sign of Nathaniel.

The front door opens and Fred steps out, holding a broom. When he starts sweeping up the rose petals, he spots Roxie. "That's a beautiful dog," he calls out. Then he recognizes Mason and me. "You're the kids from forensics camp, aren't you? Nathaniel's friends?"

"Yup," Mason says. "Hey, if you don't mind us asking, how is Nathaniel? We were supposed to hang out with him tonight, so when we didn't hear from him, we figured he was still in trouble."

Fred sets the broom down. "You had plans, did you? Well, his father has confined him to his room. I tried to reason with André—Nathaniel adores that dog, and he would never do anything to hurt his grandmother—but André told me it wasn't my place." He sighs. "I suppose Nathaniel isn't the only one in this family who needs time to get used to me."

Fred comes down the stairs so he can pet Roxie. "You look after this beautiful dog, okay?"

We promise that we will. After Fred shuts the door behind him, Mason turns to me. "I wonder what Nathaniel would say if he knew Fred was sticking up for him."

Stacey, Muriel and Nico are waiting at the corner of Lansdowne Avenue and Sherbrooke Street. "Nice to meet you, Roxie," Nico says, squatting down to shake Roxie's paw. "For the record, I'm a good guy, not a bad guy. So don't eat me."

The others have not heard from Nathaniel either. It feels strange not to have him with us—partly because we have gotten used to being six, but also because Nathaniel was so involved in the plans for tonight.

Nico and Muriel will meet our contact person. I am trying to stop calling him the dognapper—in case he isn't. Mason will hide out by the utility shed near the park entrance. From there, he will be able to see Nico and Muriel. Stacey and I will be stationed at opposite sides of the park. She will wait behind a giant recycling bin (why am I not surprised she chose that spot?). I will be crouched underneath the slide in the kids' play area.

The plan is that Mason will text Stacey and me to let us know what is going on. We have even come up with a code in case of emergency.

1=Things are fine.

2=Make a run for it.

3=Call the police.

"What about Roxie?" Mason asks. Roxie's one stand-up ear perks up when she hears her name. I think she likes it when people talk about her. "If we're going to use her for bait like Nathaniel said, she should be with me—in plain view near the entrance to the park."

I take a deep breath. "She can go with you, but only if you promise not to let her out of your sight. Not even for a millisecond," I say.

"Of course I promise."

There is a bike rack by the utility shed. "Stay," I tell Roxie as I loop her leash over the bike rack. "I'll come back for you." She looks at me with her soft dark eyes. I give her a quick scratch behind the ears. "I'm glad you understand me," I say.

It is twenty to eight—time for me to get to the play area. There is not much grass underneath the slide, just dried-up earth. I thought of this spot because when I was little I used to hide here when we played hide-and-seek. I squeeze in under the slide. It's a good thing I'm not taller, or this could get uncomfortable.

Maybe it's because I've got nothing to do or because I'm thinking about criminals that my mind takes me back again to the day of the break-in. This time I try to let the memories come without fighting them.

I see a little girl blocking her ears, then unblocking them. Then I hear a woman's voice calling for help. For a moment I think someone in the park is in trouble, but then I realize the sound is in my memory. And now I remember wondering whether there was a woman calling out on TV— or if it was Mom. The little girl blocks her ears again, like that monkey who will hear no evil. She does not want to hear. She is too afraid.

Another feeling washes over me, one I have never been aware of before when I remembered the break-in. Guilt. I didn't do anything to help my mom.

And then, for some reason I don't quite understand, I think of Larry's dog Pixie, the one he has to muzzle. Didn't Larry say some people were fear biters too? I think of how I sometimes snap at my parents, and how nasty I can be to Mason. Could I be one of those fear biters Larry was talking about? Have I been afraid all these years?

A squeegee kid walks by, drawing me back to the present. He is wearing a ratty-looking gray wool cap and carrying a backpack. He whistles, and there is something familiar about the tune, but I can't place it. What is that song? I don't think he is the contact person—he's just some kid walking through the park—but even so, I do not breathe or move a muscle. I figure it is an opportunity to practice being invisible, and it seems to be working because the squeegee kid walks right past me, still whistling.

I check the time on my cell phone. Seven fifty-five. I can feel my heart speeding up even though nothing has happened yet.

I text Mason. **Any news?**

No, he texts me back. **Just some squeegee kid walking through the park. He said "Hi pooch" when he passed Roxie.**

That is when I place the song. It's "Who Let the Dogs Out?"

TWENTY-TWO

In a big city like Montreal, I am used to seeing squeegee kids. Some have long, unwashed dreadlocks, and others' heads are shaven. Their arms are tattooed, their lips and eyebrows are pierced, and their faces are sunburned and craggy from living on the streets. They hang out at busy intersections, often at entrances or exits to the highway, and when the traffic light turns red, they rush the cars, using their squeegees to clean the windshields—even when they are perfectly clean. I have seen drivers try to wave squeegee kids away, but most drivers lower their windows just enough to hand over a buck or two.

"It's extortion," my dad says.

Mom is more sympathetic. The company she works for raises funds to help street kids, so Mom has visited some of the local homeless shelters. "I just hope those poor kids have some place to sleep tonight," my mom will say. "And what about their parents? Imagine having a child who lives on the street." Then she'll lower her window and give them some money and the address of the closest shelter.

Something else I have noticed about squeegee kids is that many of them have dogs. Dad says it is one more ploy to shake people down for money (*"You feel sorry for the poor mutt who ended up with that kid."*). Mom disagrees. I've heard her say the dogs are probably the squeegee kids' only real friends.

"Who Let the Dogs Out?"

Maybe it was pure coincidence that the squeegee kid was whistling that song. But maybe it wasn't. Could the squeegee kid be our contact person? All he would need is Internet access, which he could get at any library or coffee shop.

I text Mason. **Maybe the squeegee kid is our man.**

This time, Mason does not text back right away. All I can do is wait. I am terrible at waiting. If only I could see the bike rack from here. I imagine Roxie sitting, one ear pricked—watching and listening.

Mason texts me back. **You might be right. He's talking to Muriel and Nico now. Over and out.**

Then nothing. No more texts from Mason. My legs are getting crampy.

Except for some crickets singing and the sound of my own breathing, the park is perfectly still. I cannot stand not knowing what is going on.

So? I write to Mason.

Still no answer.

Is Roxie ok?

No answer.

A black bird—or is it a bat?—startles me when it swoops overhead. Even though the air is warm, I cannot help shivering.

And then I hear something. Words echoing in the darkness.

First a stranger's voice. Rough and angry. "You're just a kid. You should've told me. And that you were bringing a friend. I don't do business with kids."

Now Muriel's voice. Higher-pitched than usual. "So what if I'm a kid? I've got the money."

I know she does not have the money.

"Where's the dog?" That's Nico. Serious for once. Afraid. I can hear it in his voice.

"Like I said, I don't do business with kids."

And then, in the distance, a short, sharp bark. But definitely a bark—and not Roxie's, which is lower and longer. Roxie must hear the barking too, but she doesn't respond.

"Show us the Chihuahua before we give you the money." Nico's voice again. Why do they keep mentioning the money?

"Show me the money first."

The conversation stops. Now I hear the sound of a scuffle and people running. More barking. Roxie is barking now too. Someone—I can't tell who—is shouting, "Oh, crap!"

What is going on? I don't know where to look.

I jump—nearly bumping my head on the bottom of the slide—when my cell phone vibrates in my hand.

It's a message from Mason: **2**

Make a run for it.

My legs are shaking. Before I do anything else, I need to get Roxie. When I reach the bike rack, Mason is waiting for me. But where is Roxie?

I want to scream. But we agreed that no matter what, we would not draw any attention to ourselves. Besides, when I open my mouth, no sound comes out.

TWENTY-THREE

"Where is Roxie?" I hiss when my voice comes back.

"Tabitha, I don't know how to tell you—" Mason sounds like he's about to hyperventilate.

"Where is she, Mason?"

"I'm really sorry. What I'm trying to tell you is…Roxie's gone. And it's my fault."

I had been starting to appreciate things about Mason I had not noticed before, warming up to him—but not anymore. I have no sympathy for him now. "You promised, you…you…stupid jerk…" Insulting Mason does not make me feel any better. So I punch him in the stomach. But he is too pudgy to feel it. And now my knuckles hurt.

"I said I'm sorry," Mason is saying. "I messed up. I was watching the squeegee kid and Nico and Muriel. And then I had to pee—really bad. And I didn't want anyone to see me—or hear me. So I went behind that tree over there. I know I shouldn't have done it. And I swear I was only gone for a couple of minutes. Roxie was tied up, and she didn't bark or anything, so I didn't even realize until I got back."

We had a plan for what to do if things went wrong. But right now my mind can't focus on a plan. Mason follows me to the bike rack. I take my flashlight out of my pocket. In the dim light, I can see Roxie's paw prints on the dusty ground. And shoe prints too. Why would Roxie have gone with someone else anyway? Could the person have had something Roxie wanted—like a toy or a bone? I kneel down to get a closer look at the prints. It looks like whoever took her was wearing runners—old ones.

It feels like my heart is beating inside my throat. I close my eyes. Maybe that will help me think.

It is Mason who notices something glimmering on the ground: a foil candy wrapper. Could the dognapper have dropped it? Mason is about to pick up the wrapper when I stop him. "Don't tamper with the evidence," I tell him.

Then I remember I am still wearing the pink plaid shorts I wore to camp today. When I took off my rubber gloves earlier, Stacey was standing near me, and because I did not want to get a lecture about not reusing them, I stuffed them into my front pocket. I pull the gloves out now and show them to Mason. Then I slip them on, grab the candy wrapper and turn the gloves inside out so the evidence is safely stashed inside.

I am shoving the wrapper and the gloves back into my pocket when I feel a hand on my shoulder.

"Lay off!" I yell.

"It's only me."

I recognize the T-shirt—the skull and bones glow yellow in the dark—before the voice. "Nathaniel? What are you doing here?" I don't wait for an answer. "Someone took Roxie."

"Crap!" he says.

Mason shakes his head. "It's my fault. I should've been watching her."

Stacey runs over from the other side of the park. "Nathaniel? I thought you were grounded," she says.

"We heard you were locked in your room," Mason says.

Nathaniel does not bother to explain what he is doing here or how he got out of his house. "Did you see which way Nico and Muriel went?" he asks Stacey.

"Did you see Roxie?" I ask her at the same time.

"Nico and Muriel followed the squeegee kid. That way." She points north on Lansdowne Avenue to the steep part where the fancy houses are. Then Stacey looks at me. "Where's Roxie?"

"Roxie's gone. The squeegee kid must have taken her when Mason went to pee."

Stacey groans. "You went to *pee*?"

I am trying not to cry. "Roxie's been dognapped," I manage to say.

"I can't believe it," Stacey says. "But the weird thing is, I didn't see her. The squeegee kid had the Chihuahua in his backpack. But he didn't have Roxie."

"Roxie! Roxie!" I call out. I am half expecting her to bark or to come loping out of the bushes, wanting to nuzzle me, but she doesn't. The only answer I get is the rustle of the wind.

"C'mon," Mason urges us, "let's go. We need to stick together. If we catch the dognapper, he'll take us to Roxie."

"How do you know?" I ask him.

"I just know."

I decide to believe Mason, mostly because I don't have a choice. I take one last look around before I follow the others. No sign of movement except for some rustling in the tree-tops. Where in the world is Roxie? My whole body hurts from worry.

We do not wait for the light on de Maisonneuve Boulevard to turn green. We are getting to the steep section of Lansdowne when Mason whispers, "Shoot."

"What's wrong?" Nathaniel asks him.

Mason's shoulders droop. "My cell phone. I left it at the park. I put it down on the bench while I went to pee."

"Do you ever *not* forget something?" I ask him.

"We'll wait here, Mason," Nathaniel says, "but you better hurry."

"The words *Mason* and *hurry* should not be used in the same sentence," I mutter, but he gets back faster than I expect, although he's out of breath. How is he going to make it up the hill?

"I found it," he says. "And this too."

He shows us a folded-up piece of paper. When he unfolds it and holds it up to the light, we see it is a copy of the email correspondence between Muriel and the person who was trying to sell her the Chihuahua.

"Now look at this," Mason says, turning the sheet over. On the other side is another email.

"He can't be such a bad guy if he cares enough about the environment to print on both sides of a sheet," Stacey says.

The second email message is about a white standard poodle.

"I think we saw the dognapper walking through the park before," Mason says. "He's one of those squeegee kids."

Nathaniel looks up the hill. We cannot see all the way to the top of Lansdowne from here. "I just hope we haven't lost him," he says.

"What about Muriel and Nico?" Stacey asks. "Do you see any sign of them?"

"Nope. Could be they're so high up the hill we can't see them from here." The way Nathaniel says it makes me think he is trying to convince himself that there is nothing to worry about.

"I hope you realize you got your fingerprints all over that sheet," I say to Mason as we trudge up the street. But he is not listening. Neither are the others. That is because, midway up the street, someone behind a white picket fence is waving us over. Muriel.

"Where's Nico and the—?" Stacey starts to ask when we get to where Muriel is.

"Shhh!" Muriel presses her finger to her lips. "The squeegee kid went into the backyard here. Nico followed him. I said I'd wait for you guys. What took you so long?"

I want to blame Mason and tell her it's also his fault that Roxie is missing, only there isn't time. We have to find the dogs. "Let's go," I say.

"D'you think this is where he lives?" Mason asks.

"Squeegee kids don't usually live in mansions," I point out.

The lights are out and all the curtains are drawn in the house the squeegee kid has led us to. I'll bet the owners are away for the summer holidays. A long driveway leads to a three-car garage. There is another fence, a higher one, to the right of the garage. Nathaniel tries unlatching the fence from the outside, but it is locked. "They must've jumped over it," he says, stepping back so he can do the same.

Mason backs away from the fence. "Jumped over that thing? Maybe I should wait here. I could be the lookout."

"You can do it," Nathaniel says. "You jumped over a wall in the obstacle course. Besides, we'll help you."

"I don't—"

"Don't be such a girl," Nathaniel says.

"Excuse me," I say, "but did you just say what I think you said?"

Muriel and Stacey are shaking their heads too.

"That was such a sexist remark," Stacey says.

"Extremely sexist," Muriel adds. "You should know better, Nathaniel."

"I—I didn't mean it that way," Nathaniel stammers. "I just meant…look, it was a dumb thing to say."

"Should we forgive him?" Muriel asks.

"Maybe," Stacy and I say at the same time.

"Okay then, Mason," Nathaniel says, "let's do this."

Nathaniel squats down so Mason can put one hand on his back while Stacey, Muriel and I give him a boost.

"How's that for girl power?" Muriel asks Nathaniel when Mason lands on the other side of the fence.

"Okay, okay," Nathaniel says. "I said I was sorry."

Nathaniel is the next one over, and then it's my turn. When I land on the other side, Nathaniel offers me his hand, but I refuse to take it. "You never said a word about being sorry. You just said it was a dumb thing to say."

"Well then, I'm sorry," he says. "Honestly."

Once Stacey and Muriel have scaled the fence, we follow a flagstone path to the backyard. Even in the dark, the backyard is impressive. We can make out flower beds on every side and, in the middle of the yard, a giant kidney-shaped swimming pool. There is mosaic tile around the pool, and at the end where I am standing, I can see the words *DEEP END* and *NINE FEET* written out in mosaic, just like at a public pool. Behind the pool is a stone pool house, a mini version of the mansion in front.

But where is Nico? And where is the dognapper? And what about Roxie?

"Over here." It is the first time I have ever heard Nico whisper. He is crouched in front of a giant boulder. It is also the first time I have ever seen him be perfectly still.

"He went into the pool house," Nico whispers. "All we have to do is wait him out."

"D'you think he knows we're following him?" Muriel asks her brother.

"If he didn't know it before, he's probably figured it out now. You guys weren't exactly stealthy climbing the fence. I'm surprised the neighbors haven't called the cops."

When Nico says the word *cops*, the door to the pool house opens a sliver. In the moonlight, I can just make out what seem to be eyes, low to the ground, shining in the darkness. Why do they seem so familiar? Then I hear a short, sharp bark, and I realize those eyes belong to a Chihuahua.

Mason must have noticed the eyes too. "Rexford?" he calls out. "Is that you?"

It must be Rexford, because he peeks out of the pool house, looking to see who has called his name.

"Get back in here!" I hear a gruff voice say, but then Rexford makes a run for it.

Mason steps out of the shadows to grab the dog. Someone—I'm not sure who it is—says, "Watch out!"

And then everything happens so quickly, I don't know where to look.

"Now!" Nathaniel is calling. "Get him!" and Nico, Stacey and Muriel follow Nathaniel as he charges into the pool house.

"Where is he?" I hear them say.

"I can't see him!"

"D'you see him?"

"Where's your flashlight?"

"I thought you said you'd bring your flashlight!"

Mason is trying to prevent Rexford from jumping out of his arms. And someone—it has to be the squeegee kid— is making a racket behind the pool house. Staying as low as I can to the ground so he won't see me, I crawl over. The squeegee kid is hunched over the back window to the pool house, barring the shutters from the outside. That must be how he escaped without the others noticing.

I stop myself from calling out. My only advantage over him is that he does not know I am watching him.

"He's got to be in here somewhere! Maybe he's hiding under those pool noodles!" Nathaniel shouts.

Mason is still trying to hang on to Rexford. "Calm down, little fella. Lemme see if I can find some rope so I can tie you up…"

It is up to me to chase the squeegee kid. I am sure he is about to take off, and I will need to be close behind, but not so close that he will notice.

The squeegee kid dashes to the front of the pool house. What is that shiny thing he's got in his hands? A padlock! He is locking the door to the pool house so Nathaniel and the girls will not be able to get out! Our plan was to trap him in the pool house, but now he is trying to trap my friends instead!

I need to tell Mason about the back window. If he unlatches it from the outside, Nico and the girls will be able to get out, the way the squeegee kid did. But I cannot risk calling out to Mason, and if I whisper, he won't hear me. And there is no time to text him. I'll have to do it later.

My mom is always saying it is not the things we expect to go wrong that cause us the most grief. It is the unexpected things.

Mason is at the side of the pool. It looks like he's trying to cut off a piece of rope from the cord that divides the deep end from the shallow end, all the while trying to keep hold of Rexford.

My heart is pounding so hard I'm afraid the squeegee kid will hear it. My thigh muscles are tight from all the crouching I've been doing tonight. Running will feel good.

But then the thing I never would have expected happens.

The squeegee kid comes barreling into me at full force. Pushing me toward the pool. Did he know I was there all along? I am rolling too quickly to stop myself. The concrete and the flagstone slabs tear at my legs and arms. All I can think to do is bend my head forward to protect my face. The mosaic tiles are cold and hard against my skin.

Next thing I know, I am in the deep end of the pool. There's nothing I can do about my jeans and fleece hoodie, which have filled with water and are weighing me down. If only I hadn't asked Mom to take my sandals to be repaired! When I try kicking my runners off, it only makes me sink even deeper. I could drown in here! *Somebody help me, please! I need help!* But I can only scream the words inside my head, because wherever I look, all I see is water.

Bubbles. More bubbles. My head is submerged, but then, somehow, I fight my way back to the surface. I hear sounds of a skirmish. One short, sharp bark. Another body hits the surface of the water. It must be Mason.

Where is Rexford?

I sink back into the water. I've got one runner off, but I can't lose the other one.

I need to come up for air, but my clothes and that one shoe are weighing me down. Kicking makes things worse. My legs feel so heavy.

I manage to bob—but only for a second. I try to remember what Lloyd said about buoyancy, but my brain isn't working properly. When my head finally comes out of the water, I see the squeegee kid taking off. Why didn't I notice before that he is wearing army boots, not runners? So unless he pulled a Theodore Kaczynski, he can't be the one who took Roxie.

TWENTY-FOUR

I take a giant gulp of air before I sink back down. I should be afraid. But the fear only kicks in later, when I think about all the stuff that could have gone wrong.

This part is hard to admit, but Mason saves me. Not because he dives down to the floor of the pool or anything. I'm not that far gone, and he is not a strong enough swimmer for that. It is Mason's donut habit that saves me.

When I am flailing in the pool, trying to kick off my other runner and gasping for air, Mason stays buoyant. Not only that, but he manages to swim over to where I am and drag me to the side of the pool. He grabs me by my wrists, the way he dragged the dummy during the obstacle course.

I am coughing up water, and he has to clap me on the back, but thank God there is no need for mouth-to-mouth resuscitation.

"Thanks," I sputter, and pool water lands on his chin. For a second, we look at each other.

"No biggie," Mason says, though we both know that is not true. If it was not for Mason, something really bad could have happened.

"Wh-where's Rex-Rexford?" It's hard to get the words out, my teeth are chattering so bad, but Mason knows what I mean.

"He took him."

"Get us outta here!" Nathaniel bellows from inside the pool house.

"We're coming!" Mason calls back. My other runner is floating at the edge of the pool, and Mason is fishing it out.

I am trembling. Not only because I am soaking, but also because I am remembering the feeling of being weighed down underwater. I don't even want to think about what might have happened if Mason had not been there. Mason smacks my runner against the ground to get the water out. "There's a b-back w-window to the pool house," I tell Mason as I force my foot into the soggy shoe.

When we unbar the window, Nathaniel is the first one out. "Why are you guys wet?" he asks.

"He pushed me into the pool," I tell Nathaniel. "Mason got me out." I leave out the part about Mason's natural buoyancy.

Mason helps Nico and the girls out of the pool house. "Now what?" Nico says.

Stacey dusts herself off. "I think there's mildew in the pool house. Thank God you got us out of there. Many people are severely allergic to mild—"

Nathaniel cuts her off. "This isn't a good time to discuss mildew, Stacey. We need to figure out which way the squeegee kid went."

"He ran back down the path," I say.

Nico has run to the front of the house. "I think I see him," he calls back to us. "All the way down Lansdowne."

"Are you sure it's him?" Stacey asks when we get to where Nico is.

"No, I'm not sure," Nico admits. "But unless one of you has a better plan, I say we should head back down the street."

"I'm not sure this is a good idea," Stacey says.

Nathaniel grabs Stacey's elbow. "Let's go," he says. "We can argue later."

Getting down the hill is a lot easier than going up. We pass a few mansions, then an old gray-stone apartment building, then a block of townhouses. Soon we cross Sherbrooke Street and after that, de Maisonneuve Boulevard.

When we pass the park, we all turn to look. No one is there except for an older woman sitting on a bench, gazing up at the moon. "Excuse me," Muriel calls out. "Did you happen to see a guy go by, dressed in black and wearing a gray cap and carrying a backpack?"

"Does he have a dog?" the woman calls back. "Because I thought I heard a small dog yapping."

"Which way did they go?" Nathaniel asks.

"Down toward the Glen," the woman says. "Have you ever noticed how small dogs are noisier than big ones?"

I think the woman would like for us to stop and chat, but there is no time. The others are already hurrying down the street. "I've gotta go," I tell her. "But thanks."

There is a tunnel at the bottom of Lansdowne Avenue that separates Westmount, which is one of Montreal's fanciest neighborhoods, from St. Henri, which is just about the unfanciest. This is the stretch known as the Glen. It is also where Lansdowne Avenue turns into de Courcelle Street.

There is hardly any sidewalk inside the tunnel, so we walk in single file, our shoulders and hips brushing up against the damp stone wall.

"Roxie." I do not mean to say her name out loud.

Muriel reaches for my hand and squeezes it in the darkness.

"We'll find her," she says.

"Where to now?" Nico asks when we exit the tunnel.

There are several rundown buildings and some empty lots on this part of de Courcelle Avenue. Muriel is standing under a streetlamp, looking at something on her phone. The rest of us are searching for some sign of the squeegee kid. Lights flicker on, then off, in one of the rundown buildings across the street. "Maybe he went in there," Nathaniel and I say at the same time.

Stacey sniffs the air. "I smell dog—and lemon."

"Lemon?" Nathaniel asks.

Stacey sniffs a second time. "Definitely."

On Monday we might have laughed at Stacey's habit of sniffing for clues, but now we have come to respect her olfactory powers. "Where would you say those smells are coming from?" Mason asks.

Stacey does not point at the building where the lights were flickering. I gulp when she points at a building on our side of the street. It is as close to looking haunted as any building I have ever seen. It is only two stories, and most of its windows are boarded up. Though I do not know for sure that it's full of rats and spiders, I think that if I were a rat or a spider, I would want to live there. "That one," she says.

"You sure?" Nathaniel does not sound any keener than I am to explore the building.

Stacey is chewing on her lower lip. "I think it's time to call the police. Someone could get hurt. I'm starting to get super anxious." Not only is Stacey talking really quickly, but she has put her hand on her heart again. I wonder if her heart is racing like mine is.

"Take a deep breath," I tell her. "Like this." I demonstrate a breathing technique my mom taught me. In through the nose, out through the mouth. Slowly.

Stacey breathes deeply. If I had more time, I'd show her the Gyan Mudra.

Nathaniel gives Stacey a minute to collect herself. "We're not going to call the police, not yet," he tells her. "I don't want my dad to know I climbed out my bedroom window."

"You climbed out your bedroom window?" Mason sounds impressed. "Didn't you tell me your bedroom was in the attic?"

"I tied three sheets together and rappelled down. I'll show you how to do it sometime. The hard part is going to be climbing back up."

"Three sheets?" I ask. Most people only have two sheets on their beds.

"Yeah, three," Nathaniel says. "The funny thing was, Fred, my grandma's fiancé, came up to my room with fresh sheets for my bed. He's been trying to help out with the chores. Anyway, that's when I got the idea."

Mason and I exchange a look. "We ran into Fred before," I tell Nathaniel. "He didn't seem like such a bad guy."

"D'you think Fred could've been trying to help you?" Mason asks.

Nathaniel shrugs.

Muriel looks up from her cell. "Come see what I just found!"

Muriel has used Google Street View to look up this block of de Courcelle Street. Google Street View doesn't provide real-time images, so whatever Muriel is looking at is a photo that was shot some time in the past. But maybe that doesn't matter. Maybe she has found something important.

I try to move in closer, but Nico elbows his way past me so he can look at the screen first.

"In the Street View image, someone's going into the building that Stacey says smells like dog," he tells us.

"It's not just that," Muriel tells him. "Have a closer look."

Now we are all straining to get a look. I do not complain when Nathaniel steps on my toe.

That is because I just saw what Muriel already noticed. That guy going into the building on Google Street View is carrying a small dog in his arms.

TWENTY-FIVE

It would be dumb for all of us to try to get into the building. Someone needs to keep watch from outside in case anything goes wrong. I would volunteer for that job, except Roxie could be in there. If she is, I want to be the one to rescue her. Stacey offers to do guard duty. "If you're not out in exactly ten minutes, I'm phoning the police. You can deal with your dad," she tells Nathaniel.

"Make it fifteen," Nathaniel says before the rest of us head into the building.

The door is slightly ajar. It creaks when I push it open.

Stacey was right about the dog smell—and the smell of lemon. Mason points to a box on the ground. Inside are bones, the kind you can make soup from. Maybe that's what the dognappers use to lure dogs. Anger courses through my veins. Is that how the dognappers tricked Roxie into going with them?

I stop myself from calling out Roxie's name. We have agreed not to make any noise. Not unless it's absolutely necessary.

There are no walls inside the house—just rough wooden pillars. The floor is covered in sawdust. Someone must have been doing construction work in here. Muriel stops in front of a makeshift counter. On it are two tin plates, two chipped coffee mugs and a half-empty can of baked beans. There's no mold on the beans—someone must have eaten the other half of that can quite recently. For a moment I can hear my mom's voice in my head: *Imagine having a child who lives on the street.* But then I think about Roxie, and my heart hardens again.

There is a creaking noise. Someone is walking on the floor above us. We all freeze. If we can hear someone, isn't there a chance that he—or they—can hear us too? And if there are dogs in this place, where are they—and why aren't they barking?

I am standing by one of the only windows that is not boarded up. The window is streaked with grime, and there is a long crack running through it like a scar. When I hold my flashlight to the cracked glass, I see a cramped courtyard outside. Is that where they let the dogs out?

More footsteps upstairs and now voices. Two guys. One is the squeegee kid. I recognize his gruff voice from when he yelled at us by the pool. The other guy must be his accomplice. And I'll bet you anything he is wearing runners.

"How do you know they didn't follow you, Cal?" a strange voice says.

"I got rid of them, Seb. Trust me." The voice belongs to the guy who pushed Mason and me into the pool. Cal.

"Trust you? I can't believe you were dealing with some kid."

"That wasn't just any kid. That was a smart kid."

In the yellow light from my flashlight, I can see Muriel smile. Who can resist a compliment, even when it comes from a dognapper?

"We should get outta here just in case. I'll get the dogs from the basement."

The basement?

I can see my friends' eyes glimmer in the dark. My own eyes must be glimmering too. We are all wondering the same thing: How do we get to the basement first?

Upstairs, the conversation continues. "We'll never find another squat like this."

"We should leave town, Cal."

"How're we gonna leave with six dogs?"

Six dogs?

Mason waves us over to where he is standing. Without saying a word, he points with his foot to what looks like a trapdoor on the floor. And then we hear what sounds like a small dog whining.

"Willy?" Nathaniel calls out.

"Shhh," Muriel tells him, but it's too late.

The voices upstairs stop for a moment, and then I hear the guy named Seb say, "There's someone downstairs."

I can feel my heart beating in my throat. *There's someone downstairs.* Those must be the same words my mother used during the break-in at our house, and fear seeps through my veins. I need to get out of here. But then I remember that Roxie might be in the basement, and I know I cannot bolt.

What surprises me is that Mason does not take off. Roxie is not his dog—and neither is Willy. And yet there is Mason on his knees, pulling up the trapdoor, even though we can hear the dognappers coming down the stairs.

What if they try to trap us in the basement, the way the squeegee kid tried to trap the others in the pool house? I think about rats and spiders, but then I hear movement in the basement. Could that be Roxie?

I am in the basement before Mason. The stench is a million times worse than the smell of spoiled food in the cafeteria. Six dogs that no one has been cleaning up after. But, oddly, there is also something lemony in the air. And then I remember what Larry told us about the stolen bark-breaker collars. Citronella smells like lemons.

I shine my flashlight in front of me. I think I recognize the standard poodle I saw on the poster. He is sprawled out on the floor, panting. It is hard to believe his coat was ever white. He is wearing a plastic collar with a small box attached to it. The citronella must be inside.

"Roxie?" I call into the darkness.

I am answered by a whimper. That can't be Roxie.

But when I follow the sound, it leads me to her. She is whimpering because she is chained to the furnace.

I don't know if I am more angry or sad. No—I'm definitely angry. How could anyone treat dogs this way?

Roxie knows it's me, because she stops whimpering. I unlatch the chain from around her neck. "Let's get out of here," I say as she licks my face.

Nathaniel has found Willy. The Pomeranian is dancing a circle around him. Mason, Muriel and Nico are rounding up the other dogs—Rexford, the standard poodle, a Dalmatian and a sheltie.

I shine the light on the stairs as I rush back up with Roxie at my heels.

But someone is blocking my way. "What do you think you're doing?" an angry voice asks.

I could be scared. I should be scared. The person I am looking at is bigger and older than I am. Someone I have never seen before. Not the squeegee kid. This must be Seb. My eyes drop to his feet. He is wearing runners. Though I can't see the bottoms, I know the soles are worn.

If I am afraid, you cannot tell from my voice. "I'm taking back my dog," I say. "The one you stole."

"You can't prove I stole her. I'll say I just turned up here tonight. That I don't know anything about the dogs. All kinds of street kids use this place as a squat."

"We've got your footwear prints from the park," I tell him. "And we'll get your fingerprints from that can of baked beans. Plus, you dropped your emails. It shouldn't be too hard to prove you took the dogs."

"Why should I believe you?" Seb asks. "What are you—twelve years old?"

"Thirteen," I tell him.

FORENSICS SQUAD UNLEASHED

Mason is coming up the stairs with Rexford in his arms and the sheltie close behind him. Rexford squirms out of Mason's arms and makes a beeline for the door. The sheltie follows him.

The printout of the email is sticking out from Mason's front pocket. Why didn't I think of telling him to leave it with Stacey?

Seb has spotted the paper too. "It looks like you've got something of mine," he says, reaching forward to pull the sheet from Mason's pocket.

"It's all yours," Mason says. His voice is calmer than I expect.

Seb scans the sheet, then tears it up and lets the pieces fall to the floor.

"That won't help," Mason tells him. "We already took photos with our cell phones—close-up shots so we could get the fingerprints. From that sheet of paper you just tore up and from the can of beans." Mason is bluffing, of course, but Seb doesn't know that.

Muriel is coming up the stairs with the poodle. "Cell-phone photos are—"

I shoot her a look, and she stops in midsentence.

Mason reaches into his back pocket for his cell phone and makes as if he is about to hand it to Seb. "You can have my phone, if you want it. I already emailed the photos to one of our associates. For safekeeping."

Seb sneers. "Associates? What are you?" he says. "Some kind of middle-school forensics squad?"

"We're from forensics camp," Muriel says. "But now that you mention it, forensics squad sounds much cooler."

TWENTY-SIX

Leave it to Mason to start a conversation with Cal, the squeegee kid, and his accomplice, Seb. Did he forget that one of them tried to drown me thirty minutes ago?

Maybe it's because Mason does not carry grudges. After all, I have been giving him a hard time for over thirteen years, and he has never once gotten angry at me.

"So," he says, "if you don't mind my asking, how old are you guys?"

I am half expecting Seb and Cal to take off or punch us out, but I think they are so surprised Mason is talking to them in a normal way that they actually answer. Maybe Mason should become a reporter instead of a pastry chef. He has a talent for getting people to tell him stuff. "We're seventeen," Cal says. He eyes Seb, and I know they are sending each other some kind of message, only I'm not sure what the message is.

Mason has more questions. He wants to know whether they are from Montreal—Seb is and Cal isn't—and what their last names are (they won't tell him).

Nico is upstairs now too. He has brought the Dalmatian, who is snapping at the sheltie. "Shhh," Nico tells the Dalmatian, but the dog keeps snapping.

Nathaniel is still holding Willy, but I can tell from the way he is looking at Seb and Cal that he does not trust them, even if they seem to be having a calm conversation with Mason.

The poodle won't leave Muriel's side. Muriel rubs the dog's filthy coat. "Dognapping is a serious crime," she tells Seb and Cal.

"So is mistreating animals," Nathaniel adds.

Seb extends his arm the way I've seen Lloyd do. "For the record—we never mistreated those dogs. We let them out and feed them twice a day. And they get plenty of fresh water."

"Yeah, but what about the mess downstairs?" I say. "And what if they're on special diets? A lot of dogs have allergies." I almost tell them that Roxie only eats raw food. "And what about the bark breakers the dogs have on? You stole those too, didn't you?"

Cal is leaning against one of the wooden pillars. He brushes the hair out of his eyes. When he speaks, he uses the kind of voice you'd use with your best bud. "Look, you caught us red-handed and you've got evidence to prove we took those dogs. But here's a wild thought." He pauses, and when he smiles, I see that one of his front teeth is chipped. "How about you let us go? You seem like good kids. And I'm sorry about what happened at the pool." He looks at Mason and me. "I was scared. I didn't want to hurt you guys. Honest."

Mason nods. I am not so convinced Cal means it.

Nathaniel is even less convinced. "How do we know these guys aren't playing us?" he hisses.

But Cal talks over him. "Seb and I were planning to leave town once we sold the dogs. Look at it this way. You've got the dogs. That's what you wanted, isn't it? If you turn us in to the police, we'll end up in youth court, and the judge will send us to some juvie prison. I've already been, and let me tell you, it's no picnic. You can help us get another chance. Turn our lives around."

"What about the dogs you already sold?" I ask.

Cal and Seb exchange another look. "We only sold one. A wire-haired dachshund. I'll give you all the info—where she is, where we got her from—but only if you let us go." Cal is watching our faces. I can feel him gauging our reactions, trying to see if we will say yes.

"How do we know you won't leave town and start dognapping someplace else?" Muriel asks.

Seb shrugs and says, "Look at it this way. If we got caught by a bunch of middle-schoolers, I'd say it's time for us to get into a new line of work."

"A new line?" Nico asks. "Maybe you guys should try a *straight* line."

That makes Seb and Cal laugh. Cal laughs so hard he needs to clutch his belly.

Why would anyone laugh so hard at one of Nico's lame jokes? Which is how I know Nathaniel is right. These guys are playing us.

Are the others thinking the same thing? Not Nico. He is too busy laughing at his own joke. Muriel catches my eye and pats her back pocket where she keeps her phone. I think she is signaling me that she has been in touch with Stacey. Nathaniel's eyes look steely.

Mason shifts his weight from one foot to the other. I think he would like to trust Cal and Seb. "I don't know…" he whispers.

"They're playing us," Nathaniel says.

"Don't you think everyone deserves a second chance?" Mason asks.

My week at forensics camp has taught me that you can be on the same team and not agree with each other. It happens all the time. But sometimes when people on the same team disagree, it creates an opening—and trouble gets in.

Like it does now.

Seb slips behind a pillar, so that for a moment we lose sight of him. Then he dashes to the other side of the room. Nathaniel is the first of us to figure out what is happening. He rushes to the door to block Seb from leaving. Rexford wags his tail and paws at the door. The Dalmatian nips the sheltie. But Seb has another plan. He is kicking the glass in the grimy window I was looking out of before. There are jagged shards everywhere. And then Seb is gone.

"Knee—" I am trying to shout one of Roxie's commands, but Cal's hand is over my mouth. I bite his fingers, but he doesn't back off.

I need to remember what Larry taught me. Roxie is trained to respond to both verbal cues and hand signals. Cal has pinned one of my hands behind my back, but only one.

I slice the air with my free hand, and when I do, Roxie takes a run at Cal, who tries stepping away. Cal's eyes look like they are all pupil. I think he expects Roxie to jump him. Only that isn't what Roxie does. She rams into Cal's knees, just the way Larry said she would. "What the—" Cal calls out as he drops to the floor. Cal is breathing hard. Roxie uses her teeth to hold on to Cal's sleeve.

"Good dog," I tell Roxie. But it is as if she has not heard the compliment. She does not take her eyes off Cal—not even for a second. All I hear is her low growl.

Muriel grabs hold of Cal's foot, so he cannot escape. Cal tries to shake her off, but then Mason comes over and sits on Cal's stomach.

"Please, man, move. I'm begging you. I can't breathe," Cal gasps.

Mason moves—but only a little.

"I can't believe Seb took off without me," Cal mutters.

But Seb has not exactly managed to take off. About three minutes later he is back, propped up between Samantha and Lloyd. Behind them are Stacey and Nathaniel's dad.

"What are you two doing here?' Nico asks Samantha and Lloyd.

Samantha sighs. This is the first time I have ever seen her in jeans. Maybe that's why she looks younger than usual. "Let's just say we've been keeping an eye on you this evening. We got quite a workout going up Lansdowne."

Lloyd steers Seb to a small bench. "Let me see your leg," Lloyd says once Seb is sitting down. Seb does not argue. He grimaces when he extends his leg. His knee is badly cut in two places.

Nathaniel's dad rushes back to his cruiser for his medical kit.

"Hey," Seb says to Lloyd. "How do you know these kids anyhow?"

Something about the way Seb speaks to Lloyd—as if they have known each other for a long time—makes me look back and forth between them. On the surface, there is no resemblance. Seb is tall and lanky. Lloyd is smaller and wider. But they both have gray eyes and, now that I am looking closely, a bump on their noses in the exact same spot. And now I remember the conversation I overheard between Lloyd and Samantha. Lloyd said he had a brother who sometimes lived on the streets…Sebastian. Or Seb for short.

"We're their counselors. At forensics camp," Lloyd tells him.

Seb shakes his head. "You kidding me? If it weren't for this friggin' forensics camp, me and Cal would be free men."

TWENTY-SEVEN

I yawn, which makes the twins yawn, which causes Nathaniel to yawn, which makes the counselors yawn, and then Stacey and Mason end up yawning too. I wonder if there's a scientific reason yawns are contagious.

It's Friday morning, and I am so tired that when I look at the table in the conference room, I cannot help imagining how nice it would feel to fall asleep on top of it. Even without a pillow.

Stacey is passing around a sheet of paper so we can all put down our contact information. That way we'll be able to stay in touch after forensics camp.

"You mean *you're* not making the list this time?" Nico teases her.

"We're all making the list. It's a team effort," Stacey tells him.

I'm still wearing my dog-bone bracelet. I figure it's good luck. Even if the dog bone has turned green from the chlorine in the pool last night.

I was up late, filling my parents in on the dognapping case. Mom was horrified. "When I think of all the things that could have gone wrong..." she said, hugging me, then hugging Roxie.

"I'm fine, Mom, and Roxie's fine," I said, but I could tell there was still something on Mom's mind.

"Did it bring back a lot of memories for you?" she said. "Of that day?"

"You can just say *the day of the break-in*, Mom. I can handle—" I stopped myself in midsentence. I didn't mean to snap. I didn't want to be a fear biter anymore. Besides, the conversation gave me an opening to tell Mom something that had been on my mind lately.

"I should've come downstairs to help you," I whispered.

Mom looked at me hard—as if she was seeing me for the first time. "You don't mean that, Tabitha."

"I do, I do mean it. You were calling for help—and I didn't come." I couldn't look at her when I said the words.

That's when Mom put her arms around me and pulled me close. "While it was happening, there was only one thing I kept praying for—that you wouldn't leave your room," she whispered into my hair. "Thank God you didn't."

"But I could've helped you." I had to gulp to get the words out.

"You were only seven," Dad said. "There wasn't anything you could've done."

"Are you sure?" I asked them.

"We're sure," they said in unison, and suddenly I felt lighter than I had in a long time.

Of course, there was still a lot more to tell them about that night. Dad pretended to be upset about what had happened with the dognappers, but I think he was secretly proud. "You should have told us where you were going," he said. "But when I think about the courage it must have taken to follow the dognapper into that abandoned building, well, I don't know if I could have done it. Forensics camp has done good things for you, Tab. I told your mother I'm seriously considering signing up for a night class in forensics accounting. You know what they say—even old dogs can learn new tricks."

Roxie was resting at the foot of Mom and Dad's bed, but her ear pricked up when Dad mentioned old dogs.

When I went to bed, I could not fall asleep. I kept replaying the night's events in my mind. Sinking in that kidney-shaped pool. Walking into the abandoned building. Hearing Roxie's whimper. Seb shattering the window. His bloody knee. Lloyd and Samantha showing up with Nathaniel's dad.

After Nathaniel's dad had finished bandaging Seb's knee, he loaded Seb and Cal into the back of his cruiser and took them to the police station. Lloyd was going to meet them there. He told us when we got to camp the next morning that charges would be laid against the two boys. He explained to all of us that Seb was his brother. I appreciated that Lloyd was up front with us—it couldn't have been easy for him to admit his brother was involved in the dognapping.

Lloyd also told us that Cal's parents had been notified. They lived in Manitoba, but they were on their way to Montreal. They had not seen or heard from their son in nearly a year.

"As you can imagine," Lloyd told us, "I'm hoping Seb and Cal won't get sent to juvie. I'll go to court and speak on Seb's behalf. He wants to turn his life around. He says he'd like to do some kind of work with street kids and their dogs."

Nico raises his hand. "If you don't mind me changing the subject for a minute here—what about the case of the cafeteria vandal? Are we ever gonna find out who dunnit?"

"Are you saying you haven't been able to solve that case? That you guys are stumped?" Samantha asks.

"We're not stumped!" Nathaniel says. "We just got a bit distracted."

"We're aware of that," Samantha says. "And Lloyd and I want to say we're proud of you."

Lloyd wags his finger in the air. "Even though you shouldn't have been out investigating on your own. You should have spoken to us, and we'd have contacted the police, or you could have gone to the police directly."

Samantha nods, but she does not look all that upset. In fact, this is the first time in five days that I have seen Samantha smile. "Lloyd's right about that," she says, "but we still want to say you did good."

Then Lloyd and Samantha do something unexpected. They clap. For us. Which feels pretty amazing.

Nico clears his throat. "So can we get back to the cafeteria vandal—or are you two gonna keep clapping?"

Samantha smiles again. Smiling suits her. "I told you—we're getting to that. In fact, we have a special video presentation to mark the last morning of forensics camp. But before that, it's time for you guys to present the results of your forensic investigations this week."

Mason stands up. "C'mon," he says to Nathaniel. "You too. We're partners."

Nathaniel sighs, but he stands up. For once he is not slouching.

Mason starts to hum, then catches himself and stops. Public speaking makes him nervous, which is strange when you consider how comfortable he was talking to two dognappers last night. "Our handwriting analyses helped us rule out Jonah Cartwright as a suspect," he says.

"The spelling test proved inconclusive," Nathaniel adds, and then they look at each other and sit back down.

Samantha turns to Stacey and Nico. They stand up. The conference room is beginning to feel like a courtroom, and we are witnesses who are being called to testify. "You go first," Stacey whispers.

"No, you go," Nico whispers back.

Then they both start speaking at once. "Our footwear impressions indicated that three of the suspects were in the cafeteria kitchen—Mrs. Lu, Leo Tessier and Amelia Lester," Nico is saying.

"We did not find Jonah Cartwright's footwear impressions," Stacey says, though it is hard to hear her over Nico.

"Fingerprint team?" Lloyd says to Muriel and me.

Muriel and I stand up, and she does not ask if I want to go first. She just starts rattling off information. "We found fingerprints belonging to Mrs. Lu on the counter and freezer. Unfortunately, we were unable to get fingerprints from the mustard container. However, we were able to establish that there was mustard inside a coffee cup that was found next to the mustard container. We found two fingerprints on that coffee cup. One of those fingerprints belongs to Leo Tessier. The other one is Amelia Lester's."

If I do not speak up, Muriel may not let me get a word in. So I add, "We were hoping to have a little more time this morning to gather some additional evidence."

"Additional evidence?" Samantha checks the time on her cell. "I'm afraid that won't be possible. Because we're expecting some guests for the screening of our video."

As if on cue, there is a knock on the conference-room door, and Mrs. Lu comes in with Jonah Cartwright, Leo Tessier and Amelia Lester.

Mrs. Lu gives us a quick bow. "Good morning, forensics students."

Jonah Cartwright waves. Leo Tessier says, "*Bonjour,*" and Amelia Lester says, "Good morning. I hope none of you skipped breakfast. Many nutritionists believe breakfast is the most important meal of the day." At first I think Amelia is being serious, but then she winks.

"In France, we like to have ham with our breakfast," Leo says, and I know he is trying to goad Amelia. This morning she doesn't squabble with him, just rolls her eyes.

Samantha and Lloyd are setting out extra chairs for our guests.

"We were hoping our campers would be able to solve the case of the cafeteria vandal," Lloyd tells the visitors, "but it appears that hasn't happened."

"Don't forget to mention that we helped solve a real case," Nathaniel calls out.

"I heard all about it from Samantha and Lloyd. I'm very impressed," Leo Tessier says, and I can tell from the way the others look at us that they are impressed too.

Samantha slides the DVD into the computer. It's another homemade movie, like the one where the four suspects were interviewed.

It is hard to tell where the first scene is set. It's some-place dark, and whoever is filming is moving the camera around in a way that makes me dizzy.

Now we are looking at the too-strong light from a streetlamp. And then, suddenly, we see the entrance to the Life Sciences Building.

Someone is walking into the building. But because we see the person from behind, it is hard to know who it is.

"That's Jonah Cartwright," Stacey calls out. "I can tell from how fast he walks and from his jean jacket."

When the person opens the door to the Life Sciences Building, he turns to face the camera. Stacey was right. It's Jonah.

"What's he doing going into the building at night?" Nico asks.

"Didn't we rule him out as a suspect?" Mason wants to know.

"Shhh," Muriel tells them.

Jonah is speaking into the camera. "I'm on my way to return a library book," he says, holding a book up in the air so we can see it. The book is called *The History of Student Protest.* "There's a drop box in the lobby."

The camera trails Jonah as he leaves the building.

Now we see that Mrs. Lu is in the lobby. She has one of those buckets with wheels at the bottom and a mop attached to the side.

"I look terrible," Mrs. Lu says. "Like an old lady."

"She *is* an old lady," Nico whispers. Muriel whacks her brother's elbow.

"Ow!" Nico groans. "Why are you always trying to hurt me?"

"Because you're an idiot," she tells him.

"Muriel, Nico, settle down, please," Samantha says.

On the video, Mrs. Lu is rolling her bucket down the hallway to the cafeteria. There are two shadowy figures in the distance, and they seem to be arguing—Leo Tessier and Amelia Lester.

Samantha yawns. "Excuse me," she says, but then she yawns again. Which sets off another chain reaction of yawning.

Which is when I get an idea. "Excuse me," I say as politely as I can. "Do you think maybe we could pause the DVD so I could go downstairs and get some coffee—for the adults?" My eyes meet Muriel's for a second. She knows what I am up to.

"To tell you the truth, I'd give my life for a coffee," Amelia says.

"An excellent idea." Leo Tessier pronounces *excellent* the French way.

Mrs. Lu shakes her head. "I don't drink coffee. Green tea only."

Muriel and I exchange another look.

"Um…" I take a breath. I need to make it sound like the question I am about to ask is no big deal. "How do you guys take your coffee?"

"One sugar for me," Samantha says.

"Black," Lloyd says.

I look over at Leo and Amelia.

"In France, people who really know their coffee—like *moi*—never use sugar."

Amelia rolls her eyes at her boss. "I'll have three sugars," she says. "Thank you very much."

"Thank *you* very much," I say to her. "And by the way"—now I am looking at everyone sitting around the table—"we've just decided who our prime suspect is."

"We have?" Nico says.

I turn back to Amelia. "You vandalized the cafeteria, didn't you, Amelia Lester?"

Amelia Lester puts her hands on her cheeks. "I, uh, don't know what to say." She looks over at Samantha and Lloyd.

When she speaks, Samantha's voice is perfectly level. "There's no need to say anything. What we need to do is watch the rest of the DVD—after Tabitha comes back with those coffees."

There is no lineup at the coffee shop when I get there. "Triple sugar?" the guy at the counter says when I give him the order. "Let me guess. That one's for the assistant chef, right?"

When I get back to the conference room, the others are passing around a giant bowl of popcorn. While I was gone, Lloyd remembered there was a bag of popcorn in the supply closet, and he microwaved it.

I grab a handful of popcorn and settle in to watch the end of the DVD.

On the screen, Mrs. Lu walks into the cafeteria kitchen. She wipes down the counters and mops the floors. Then she surveys the room, and we hear her talking to herself. "Nice and clean," she says. "You do good work, Mrs. Lu." Before she leaves, she runs one hand along the counter—as if she is checking to see whether it is dry.

"That's when she must have left her prints," Muriel says.

On her way out of the kitchen, Mrs. Lu runs into Leo and Amelia. They are each carrying a paper coffee cup. "What you two doing here? Cafeteria closed," she tells them.

"We often come in at night to get an early start. We're trying out a new recipe. For vegetarian chili," Amelia tells her, stressing the word *vegetarian*.

"I prefer it with beef myself," Leo mutters.

"Floor may still be wet," Mrs. Lu warns the pair before she disappears down the corridor with her rolling bucket.

We watch as Amelia sets her coffee cup on the edge of the counter. Leo wants to put his cup down too, but he needs to push Amelia's cup away to make room for his. As the two of them get to work, all we hear is the sound of their knives as they chop onions and green peppers.

"Beef adds flavor to chili," Leo says.

Which is when the argument begins. Amelia lays her knife down on the counter. "Why are you so obsessed with meat? Don't you see how many of our customers are vegetarian or vegan? Don't you care about the planet?"

"She's right about the planet," Stacey whispers.

"How dare you speak to me like that!" Leo says to Amelia. "I am your boss."

"Not if I quit!" she tells him.

"You cannot quit. What would I do without an assistant?"

"I *will* quit," she tells him. "Unless you add more vegetarian options to the menu."

"This is blackmail!" Leo shouts. "I am leaving here now. You can make your vegetarian chili without me—and without meat!"

Leo grabs his coffee cup and storms out.

At first Amelia just continues chopping. But then she puts down her knife again and looks into the camera. "I've had it," she says.

She uses a kitchen towel to open the freezer and then starts emptying its contents onto the floor. When the freezer is empty, she reaches into the fridge for the mustard container. She squeezes the container, but the opening is blocked. When she unblocks it with her fingers, a little wad of mustard flies up into the air and lands in her coffee cup. As she leaves her mustard message on the counter, we hear her say to herself, "Writing with a squeeze bottle sucks."

When Amelia tosses the mustard container into the garbage, she makes a noise that sounds like a battle cry.

ACKNOWLEDGMENTS

I could not have written this book without Rachel Rudolf, who told me about the forensics day camp at the University of Toronto, Mississauga campus. Rachel also spent several days with me at the camp in July 2014, answered many questions about forensics and read an early draft of this story. Thanks also to Tracy Rogers, director of the University of Toronto's Forensic Science program, for letting me attend camp for a week, and to forensic-anthropology students and counselors Tori Berezowski and Danielle Stoewner for being smart and fun and putting up with my many questions. Special thanks to the kids I met at camp—for sharing their love of forensic science and for not minding having a curious, noisy adult around all week: Ben Allday, Isaiah Chidambaram, Lavinia Contreras, Harriet Dolenko, Michael D'Onofrio, Katherine Fay, Patrick Kuo, Monica Lamacchia, Sophie Mahan, Anthony Marchetta, Alexandra Markiewicz, Callum McDonell, Christian Palermo, Kyle Rakoczy, Delaney Ras, Jacob Russo, Megan Shih, Zoe Szabo, Mason Vaccari, Megan Wahl and Wan Yun Xue. Thanks also to my friend Viva Singer for her expertise about all things dog related and for letting me talk through another story with her. Finally, many, many thanks to the entire team at Orca, especially my editor and friend, Sarah Harvey, for her wise guidance.

She tosses her coffee cup into the garbage too. Then, at the very last second, just as the DVD ends, she reaches under the deep fryer for the grease trap—and grins into the camera.

TWENTY-EIGHT

There is pizza for lunch, and our visitors stay for some too. Lloyd and Samantha have ordered four jumbo pizzas—two vegetarian and two all-dressed. I keep expecting Leo and Amelia to get into another fight, but then I remember that all that conflict between them was just part of a performance. They may disagree when it comes to their philosophies of food, but they seem to get along fine in the real world.

Camp ends early today. I hate saying goodbye, so instead I ask for permission to use the photocopier so I can make us each a copy of the list with our contact information.

Lloyd shakes our hands. I figure Samantha will shake our hands too, but at the last second she seems to reconsider and gives us each a hug. And then they are off.

The six of us linger a little longer in the lobby of the Life Sciences Building.

The guy from building services waves when he sees us. "You are just the people I was looking for."

"We are?" Nico says.

The man takes a white envelope out of his shirt pocket. "Someone dropped this off for you guys this morning."

He hands me the envelope. Inside is a letter—and a crisp one-hundred-dollar bill.

I read the letter to the others.

"I am writing to thank you from the bottom of my heart for rescuing my beloved Rexford. The police told me that the six of you have been attending a forensics camp at the University of Montreal. If I was still a kid, I'd go to a camp like that myself. You have made me very happy by finding Rexford for me. Please find enclosed the one-hundred-dollar reward that I promised. Sincerely yours, Ada Dell."

Muriel has already whipped out her cell phone and is dividing one hundred by six. "That's sixteen dollars and sixty-six cents for each of us," she says. "More or less."

Mason has a different idea. "Why don't we donate the money instead?"

Nico slaps his knee. "Hey, I just got a better idea—you can donate it to me!"

"What if we donate it to a shelter for homeless teen-agers?" Mason says.

Even Nico has to admit that's a good idea.

"My mom will know which shelter needs it most," I tell the others.

Once that is settled, we head out of the building.

In the distance, I can see an older couple with a small dog walking toward us. When the dog stops to poop, the man leans over to scoop it up with a plastic bag. You can see from

MONIQUE POLAK

the way the man moves that reaching down makes his joints ache. But then he reaches down again to pat the dog's head.

It is only when we get a little closer that I realize the dog is Willy, and the people are Nathaniel's grandmother and her fiancé, Fred.

Nathaniel is on the sidewalk next to me. When I look at him, I can tell he is watching the couple and the dog too. They are at the curb, and Fred takes Nathaniel's grandmother's arm and helps her back up to the sidewalk. She smiles up at him, and Willy barks. He has recognized Nathaniel.

"Hey, Willy!" Nathaniel calls out. "Hey, Grandma." Then he pauses a little longer and calls out, "Hey, Fred!"

Nathaniel's grandmother lets Willy off his leash, and the Pomeranian comes prancing over to us. If he was traumatized from being dognapped, he seems to have made a full recovery.

"We were hoping we'd run into you," Fred says. "The bakery called. Our wedding cake is ready. They made an extra cake with the same batter and frosting, and they invited us to come and sample it. There should be more than enough if all of you kids want to join us. What do you say?"

Nathaniel is squatting on the ground. Willy is dancing on his hind legs again. "I say yes," Nathaniel says slowly.

"What flavor cake is it?" Mason asks.

"Double chocolate with buttercream frosting," Nathaniel's grandmother says.

The eight of us—nine, if you count Willy—head for the bakery together.

Mason and I end up walking side by side. He gives me a nudge. I figure he wants to discuss double chocolate cake. But I figured wrong, because instead he says, "Hey, I'm sorry I didn't do a good job of watching Roxie last night. It was my fault the dognappers got her."

"Apology accepted," I tell him, reaching out to shake his hand. "Besides, everything worked out okay. But I just want to make one thing clear, Mason. Next summer, I don't want to go to cake camp or pottery camp or tennis camp or whatever weird camp our parents have planned. I want to go to the advanced-level forensics camp. And I think you should come too."

Forensics Squad Unleashed is Monique Polak's nineteenth novel for young people. Monique is a two-time winner of the Quebec Writers' Federation Prize for Children's and Young Adult Literature. She has taught English and humanities at Marianopolis College in Montreal for thirty years. She is also an active freelance journalist whose work appears regularly in the *Montreal Gazette* and in Postmedia newspapers across the country. In 2014, Monique spent a week at the University of Toronto's forensics camp, doing research for this novel. Monique lives in Montreal. For more information, visit www.moniquepolak.com.